THE CHRISTMAS INHERITANCE

Amish Romance

BRENDA MAXFIELD

Tica House Publishing

Sweet Romance that Delights and Enchants!

Personal Word from the Author

Dearest Readers,

Thank you so much for choosing one of my books. I am proud to be a part of the team of writers at Tica House Publishing who work joyfully to bring you stories of hope, faith, courage, and love. Your kind words and loving readership are deeply appreciated.

I would like to personally invite you to sign up for updates and to become part of our **Exclusive Reader Club**—it's completely Free to join! We'd love to welcome you!

Much love,

Brenda Maxfield

VISIT HERE to Join our Reader's Club and to Receive Tica House Updates!

https://amish.subscribemenow.com/

Contents

Chapter One

The lines are fallen unto me in pleasant places;
yea, I have a goodly heritage.

— PSALMS 16:6 KJV

Caleb Ebersole set down the shammy cloth after dusting their newest buggy. It was December now, and he hoped more than one customer would be looking for a new buggy to end the year or to start the new one. His grandfather, Vernon, who owned the shop, claimed December was a good business month. Caleb hoped this year would be no exception. He'd like to have good news to report. Maybe that would raise his grandfather's spirits and give him some gumption to feel better—maybe even to get up from his bed to join the family for a meal or two.

Caleb looked over the showroom. They had four buggies in stock, but they could order more and have them delivered in good time. Vernon had made solid friends with his suppliers over the years, and they did well by him.

The shop phone rang and their secretary and general helper, Shannon Zook, answered it in her clear, friendly voice. "Ebersole's Buggies. How may I help you?"

Caleb moved to the small office at the back of the shop. He had November's figures ready for her grandfather's perusal. They had made a decent profit, even though it wasn't quite as good as November the year before. But last year had been unusually good to them, for which Caleb thanked God.

He glanced up and saw Shannon hurrying toward him. Though she carried some extra bulk on her middle-aged frame, she moved quickly. "Caleb... That was a call from the phone shanty. Your *groosdaadi*... He wants you. You need to hurry."

"What?" Immediate alarm zapped through him. Grandfather wouldn't bother him in the middle of shop hours. "Who was it you talked to? Who called?"

"It was your *dat*. He said to hurry." The worried look on Shannon's face spoke volumes.

Caleb grabbed his coat from the back of his chair and pulled it on as he hurried from the office. "Can you mind the store for me?"

"Of course," Shannon answered, pushing her glasses further up the bridge of her nose, following him across the floor. "Hurry now."

Caleb had unhitched the wagon for the day of work, but once outside, he made quick time hitching it back up. Within a few minutes, he was on the road. He snapped the reins. "C'mon, Bessie! Hurry now. C'mon," he urged.

The buggy shop was only two miles from home, where his grandfather lived in the *daadi haus*. His grandmother had died a good ten years before, and Vernon lived out there by himself, even though Caleb's folks tried to convince him to take a bedroom in the main house. But Vernon wouldn't have it. He liked his independence, he stated in no uncertain terms.

Independence. What a thought, one that wasn't too familiar with anyone in their Amish district.

Why would his *groosdaadi* want him right then? Had he taken a turn for the worse? He'd seemed fine at breakfast that morning when Caleb had toted his meal out there. For though Vernon wouldn't sleep in the big house, he did accept meals taken out to him three times a day. That morning, he'd greeted Caleb like normal. Nothing had seemed amiss—to Caleb's eyes at least.

When the farm came into sight, Caleb snapped the reins again, feeling a growing dread. He pulled Bessie to a halt and jumped out of the buggy, taking off at a run around to the *daadi haus* behind the main house. He flew through the door.

"I'm here," he called out.

His mother emerged from Vernon's bedroom. Her expression was steeled, and her voice tight. "He's … he's convinced this is it."

"What do you mean?" A cold hand gripped Caleb's heart.

"He's convinced he's dying," she said, and her voice caught. "He wants to see you … alone. I'll go get your brother. And Lloyd."

"Where is *Dat*?"

"I don't know." Tears filled her eyes. "They were here and then left to call you. I'll find him and Ephraim both. Go on in now. We'll be waiting until you're done."

Caleb squared his shoulders and walked tentatively into his grandfather's bedroom. Vernon Ebersole sat propped in bed, his eyes sharp, but his mouth sagging slightly. His thin cheeks were taut, and his gray hair was sparse and mussed, sticking up at odd angles. His bony fingers moved restlessly at the edge of the quilt which was pulled over his frail body. Caleb's eyes widened, not understanding such a fast deterioration from only a few hours before.

Had Caleb missed it? Had he been paying so little attention to his grandfather that morning? Had he been so distracted by what he was going to do that day in the shop?

"*Daadi*," he said, moving close.

Vernon patted the side of the bed. "Sit."

His voice was still surprisingly strong for his appearance. Caleb carefully perched on the side of the bed.

"I wanted to talk to you alone," he said. His eyes darted to the side of the room. If Caleb didn't know better, he'd think his grandfather was avoiding his gaze somehow. But, of course, that would make no sense ... until he spoke again.

"I want to talk to you about the shop."

Caleb tensed. It had been understood for years that the shop would go to Caleb when Vernon succumbed. Caleb was the only one who was interested in the running of it. He'd poured his heart and soul into it just as his grandfather had done. He loved the shop. He loved the buggies. He loved dealing with the customers.

But now, hearing his grandfather's tone, he instinctively knew something was wrong. But what could it be? He knew the shop's finances inside and out. They were solid. Viable. It was a good business. They weren't in trouble.

"What is it, *Daadi*?"

Again, Vernon averted his gaze. Caleb stiffened. What was it? What was wrong?

"Ephraim is having trouble..." He paused.

It was true. Caleb's younger brother was unfocused these days, causing his folks no small amount of worry. Ephraim didn't like farming. In truth, he didn't seem to like anything he tried his hand at. He claimed to still be in his *rumspringa*, though it should have ended long ago. Ephraim was twenty-six years old—plenty old enough to have joined church and settled down into his life's work.

"I know he is. But he's Ephraim." Caleb shrugged. "He'll settle down soon enough."

Caleb tried to sound sure and even a bit light-hearted about it, but it didn't work. Instead, his voice sounded tentative. Doubtful.

Vernon shook his head and waved his thin arm through the air, as if dismissing Caleb's words.

"He ain't like you," Vernon said. "He needs something. I'm not long for this world. *Gott* is tapping me on the shoulder. I don't know how much longer I'll be aware or even awake." He sucked in a huge breath.

"Surely not, *Groosdaa*—" Caleb tried to disagree, but Vernon wasn't having it. Again, he made an impatient movement with his arm.

"While I still got time, I want to help the boy."

Caleb felt his jaw tighten as alarm coursed through him. What was his grandfather going to do? Caleb felt like plugging his ears and singing at the top of his lungs so as not to hear him. But, of course, he didn't. He sat obediently; his eyes glued to his grandfather's face.

"If he had some purpose, it would do him good." Vernon paused here to cough and sputter before going on. "I want him to have the shop." He wiped a bit of spittle from his lower lip. "It will save him."

Caleb took a quick, sharp breath and gritted his teeth. Anger choked him, and he worked to control himself. *Ephraim* get the shop? Ephraim who didn't care one fig about it? Ephraim who'd rather go off with his *Englisch* friends than work for even one hour? Ephraim had never shown any interest in the shop at all.

A cold knot formed in Caleb's stomach, and he staggered to his feet. *"What?"*

"You're angry," his grandfather said. "I understand. But it must be done. The shop will save him. He'll ... he'll step up."

"*Nee!* He won't!" Caleb sank to the bed again, grabbing his grandfather's bony hand. "He'll destroy it. All your life's work, gone. I tell you, *Daadi*, this isn't—"

"Enough," Vernon sputtered out the word, and Caleb immediately saw the toll this conversation was taking on him. "You will help him."

Caleb's eyes widened. *No.* There was no way he was going to do that. The shop should be his. He'd worked there for years. He'd helped build it into what it was today. Stay and help his brother? No.

"Promise me…" Vernon said, his voice weakening. "Promise me…"

Caleb stared at him, not believing any of this was real. It couldn't be real. It just couldn't.

Vernon's eyes sat like two dark coals in his head, piercing into Caleb until he had to look away. Promise his grandfather? How could he do that? And how could this possibly work? It was unfathomable. His grandfather must be losing his mind.

A strangled sigh left Vernon's lips and Caleb tensed. "*Daadi? Daadi,* are you all right?"

His eyes were closed now, and his breathing was somewhat ragged. Alarmed, Caleb ran into the front room where his mother and father and brother were waiting. They immediately jumped to their feet.

"Is he… Is he…?" his mother asked.

"He's asleep, I think," Caleb said.

Caleb stood still as the rest of his family rushed into Vernon's room. Caleb went to the couch and sank onto it, his mind and his heart reeling. How could this be happening? He'd thought his grandfather would be around for years to come. When he'd taken to his bed a month ago, Caleb expected every week would be the one when he would get up and come back to work. Certainly by Christmas, he'd be fine again. Caleb never ever thought this would be the end.

But now...?

Caleb felt sick to his stomach. He felt betrayed by the man he admired most in the world. How could he have pulled Caleb's very life out from under him?

Caleb worked to swallow the bitter taste that filled his mouth. And he was acutely, painfully aware he hadn't promised his grandfather anything.

Chapter Two

Ruth Riehl tied the last wind chime onto the hanging display in her tiny shop. She couldn't resist giving it a gentle push as if the wind were passing by. She was rewarded by the gentle tinkling of the chime, not unlike water trickling over smooth round stones in a bubbling stream. She smiled with contentment. It was just the sound she'd hoped for when she'd made it. She was getting better and better at this, and her growing sales seemed to confirm the fact. It didn't hurt that it was coming on Christmas in a few weeks. The influx of customers had increased until she was busy pretty much from the minute she opened her shop until the minute she turned the sign over to *Closed*.

In truth, she was glad she'd worked so hard lately to beef up her inventory. She'd made so many wind chimes in the early fall, her fingers had grown calloused and sore. But her efforts were paying off now.

The small chime above her door sang out as another customer came in. Ruth smiled when she saw Annie Zookerman, her best friend.

"Hello, Annie."

Annie grinned and reached up, trailing her fingers along the hanging chimes, filling the shop with a chorus of sound. "Hi, Ruth."

"What are you doing here, today?" Ruth asked.

"Can't I come visit my friend when I want to?" Annie walked over to her.

Ruth laughed. "Of course, you can."

Annie grew sober. She glanced around the small shop as if looking for another customer who might be lurking somewhere. Seeing no one, she went on. "I wanted to warn you."

Ruth's brow rose. "Warn me? About what?"

Annie shifted her weight from one foot to the other. "Umm. Well..."

"What is it?" Ruth asked, growing alarmed. "Has something happened?"

"Not really." Annie bit her lip and then continued. "It's about Robert Blank."

Ruth blanched. She had no interest whatsoever in hearing about Robert Blank. Ever since he'd broken their engagement and run off with an *Englisch* nurse, she had considered him merely a left-over figment of her imagination. But now, hearing his name from Annie's lip, she was reminded once again that he did indeed exist—that he was very much alive and well.

Her entire body tensed as she asked, "What is it?"

"I know you don't want to talk about him." Annie's sympathy nearly made Ruth want to cry, but she forced her emotions back. "And I don't blame you, but you'll find out soon enough." Here, Annie took a deep breath. "He's back, visiting his grandparents. He's brought *her* with him, and she's ... well ... she's with child."

Ruth fumbled behind her until she felt her stool and sank down on it. The fact that Robert—after rejecting his faith by marrying an *Englischer*—could still be welcome to visit his Amish kin, disturbed her. But as he hadn't yet joined church before he'd run off, he was still welcome. He'd been two weeks short of joining church, for their engagement couldn't be official until he did. But even so, their engagement had been very official in Ruth's heart.

And now, he was back. And with his pregnant wife?

With effort, Ruth squared her shoulders. "I ... see."

Annie stepped close and put her arm around Ruth's shoulders. "I thought you should know, in case, well, in case you run into him and ... *her*."

"Thank you," she said, and she was grateful, she supposed. But hearing Robert's name brought it all back in a rush. The memories, the feelings, the embarrassment, all of it. She braced herself against it, wondering how long it was going to stay in her mind. How long was it going to stay in her heart? She didn't want it. Didn't want any of it.

She slid off her stool. "Did you see my newest wind chime?" she asked, her voice unnaturally bright. "Right there." She pointed. "What do you think of it? I cut the aluminum at an angle for this one."

Annie looked up at the wind chime and nodded and then turned her gaze back to Ruth. "It's nice," she said. Ruth could hear how sorry Annie was for all of it—for everything that had happened. Particularly since it was Ruth's second broken engagement. Of course, with Matthew, it had been completely different. Poor Matthew had died from leukemia, and his tragic loss still haunted Ruth in the middle of the night.

Ruth sighed, and she and Annie stared at one another for a long moment.

"Ruth," Annie said softly, "someday you'll find your perfect husband. It will happen. I know it will."

Ruth's eyes filled with sudden tears, which she impatiently wiped away. "Maybe," she finally said.

"No maybe about it." Annie smiled then, and grabbed Ruth's hand, squeezing it. "You want to go to the next youth sing with me? It's this Sunday evening."

Everything within Ruth wanted to say no, but she feared Annie would then make it her mission to get her to agree.

"I might."

Annie beamed. "*Gut.* I'll talk with you about it some more at preaching service."

Ruth nodded, wishing now that Annie would leave. Two customers came into her shop at that very minute. Annie let go of her hand, waved good-bye and left the shop.

It wasn't real. It couldn't be. Vernon Ebersole couldn't be dead. But he was. Even now, his body was in the open casket in the front room for viewing. People from miles around had come, parading through the room, sharing stories and anecdotes from Vernon's life. Caleb's mother stood stoically; a smile painted on her face while blinking her red, puffy eyes. His father stood at her side, a silent pillar for her to lean on if needed.

And Ephraim? Where was he? Here and then gone. And then back again for a few minutes and then gone again. Caleb took his position at the entrance of the house, diligently greeting their guests and laughing politely at their jokes and memories. He hadn't moved in hours. Tomorrow was the funeral, and he prayed for decent weather. It wasn't easy to dig a grave in the frozen December ground.

"I s'pose you'll be taking over the shop now," Zach Wittmer said as he entered the house.

Caleb worked to keep his expression neutral. "I've been there for years," he said, not answering the man. But Zach didn't seem to notice; he simply went on to tell Caleb how much he liked his latest buggy purchase, bragging on the quality of inventory Vernon always had available. Caleb nodded, his heart breaking.

He hadn't promised his grandfather what he'd asked, which ate at his conscious. At first, he hoped no one even knew what his grandfather had planned. If no one knew, then Caleb could simply continue his work at the shop as before. But it hadn't worked out that way, and in any case, Caleb supposed he'd have too much guilt about it to carry on.

Two days after his conversation with his grandfather, Vernon had passed. He never did wake up. He never said another word to anyone. Caleb would have to carry that with him for the rest of his life. He wondered if he would have been more amenable, or if he had promised to do as his grandfather wished immediately, if Vernon would have rallied. But there was no way to ever know that now. It was over, and his grandfather was dead and gone.

Caleb's mother had found the letter written by Vernon the day after he passed. It was in the drawer of his bedside table, and she read it to the whole family, her voice breaking with every phase.

Dear Family,

If you're reading this, I am dead and hopefully, I have gone to my reward. It is my dearest wish that Gott welcome me to heaven. I want to see my Mary again.

I'm assuming we've all said our gut-byes. I've had a fine life, and I don't carry regrets. Gott has been gut to me and to all of us, and for that, I am grateful.

I plan to speak to Caleb about the buggy shop. He'll likely have already told you what I'm going to say. I am giving the shop to Ephraim. I know Caleb has worked faithfully in the shop for years, and he's a gut boy. He'll be fine no matter what he chooses. But I am doing this for Ephraim. I know he'll rise to it and do the job well. Caleb will be there to guide him.

I'm tired. I don't want to write anymore. I love all of you. We don't make a habit of saying it, but we know it.

Vernon

. . .

When she had finished reading, Ephraim jumped out of his chair and began pacing back and forth. "What? Why'd he do that?" he cried. "I never asked him for it, Caleb. You gotta believe me."

Caleb had sat stony-faced. "I know you didn't," he said, again feeling sick to his stomach.

"Why'd he do that? I don't want it. I don't want it, I tell you." Ephraim's face screwed up into a grimace, and his eyes darted from his mother to his father to Caleb. "I don't want it."

Bernice had burst into tears at that, pressing the letter to her chest. Lloyd stood and grabbed Ephraim by both his arms.

"That's enough," he said, his voice sharp "This was your *daadi's* legacy. You'll take it and with gratitude. Do you hear me? It's yours now. You make him proud."

Bernice stifled another sob, and Ephraim gave her a piteous look.

Lloyd shook his son's arms. "Enough acting like a spoiled *kinner*. We didn't raise you this way. You just got something big. Something special."

Bernice stood up then and went to the window, her back facing them. But Caleb could see by her shaking that she was still crying. He knew she was hurt that Ephraim didn't respect what his grandfather had done for him.

Caleb swallowed past his own anger. Did *he* respect what his grandfather had done? No. He didn't. It was highly unjust. He stared at his brother, trying to curb his resentment. And now, he would have to help Ephraim run the shop—there was no hiding from that, either.

Lloyd let go of his son and Ephraim sank onto a rocking chair. The chair creaked on the wooden floor. Ephraim's lips were tight, and he gazed down at his hands.

Lloyd sighed heavily and sat down beside Caleb. "You'll help him."

Caleb brought his gaze to his father's and saw the certainty in his father's gaze. How was it that his father acted as if this didn't cut Caleb to the core? How was it that his father thought this was all right with him?

When Caleb didn't respond, his father's jaw visibly tightened. "You'll help him?" This time when he said it, there was a kernel of doubt in his tone.

Caleb shrugged, not trusting himself to answer at first. Then he drew in a deep breath. "I don't know." The words were out before he could stop them. The room went eerily silent. Then Ephraim made a small choking noise.

"See?" Ephraim said. "Caleb should have the shop. What was *Daadi* thinking? I'm giving it to you, Caleb."

The tightening in Caleb's chest began to open, but his father stopped that right quick.

"*Nee*, you won't. We'll follow your *daadi's* wishes. He had reasons for what he did. We're going to honor them."

Ephraim stood up. He glanced at his mother's back and then turned to his father. "*Nee*. It's Caleb's shop. It has been for a long time now. I won't take it away."

Lloyd sprang to his feet. "You'll do as you're told, son. You'll do as your *daadi* wished. Come Monday morning, you'll be there. And Caleb? You'll be there helping him. You hear me, both of you? I won't have this, I tell you."

Caleb stood and gave his father a searing stare and stalked from the room. He burst through the front door and out onto the cold porch. He stood at the top of the steps and gulped in a huge frigid breath. There was a smattering of snow on the ground, with patches of dry grass poking through.

He tried to steady his breathing. A white Christmas this year, no doubt. The snow would begin in earnest any day now. But then, being Indiana, one never knew for sure. It could warm up to spring temperatures at any time. Caleb gripped the railing, feeling the cold penetrate his skin.

How was he to do this? How was he to watch his brother bumble along, possibly destroying everything he and Vernon had built?

You have to help him, he told himself. *You have to help him and then stand back and let him take over the business you love.*

He'd dreamed of inheriting the business one day—and courting a lovely girl and marrying and then depending on the shop for their livelihood. It was a beautiful dream, one that he enjoyed many times a week. Often, he dreamt of it right before he went to sleep.

He didn't have the girl chosen yet; although, there were a few girls who had caught his interest. Not enough to pursue any of them, but still...

And now? Now what did he have to offer? Would he have to start all over in another business? Did he have to take up farming? His nostrils flared. He didn't like working the land. Oh, he'd done it for years as a youngster, helping his father. But once Vernon let him work at the shop, farming was no longer a part of his life, and he was glad for it.

Did he have to take it back up now—in hopes he'd inherit the farm and could work it to support his family?

Or would his brother keep him on at the shop in some sort of assistant position? Caleb let go of the railing, and his fist curled into a ball. He loved his grandfather dearly, but right then, had he still been alive, Caleb would have confronted him in no uncertain terms.

This wasn't right.

It just wasn't.

Caleb hurried down the steps and strode across the yard toward the barn.

Chapter Three

Ruth put on her best navy-blue dress and a fresh *kapp*. She picked up the hand mirror on her dresser and gazed at herself. All she saw were her eyes. They stared back at her, and she clearly saw the depth of hurt in them. Why in the world did Robert have to come back to town? And flaunt his pregnant wife no less? Why couldn't they have stayed put in Linder Creek, where she knew they'd moved.

The very fact that she knew where they'd moved was annoying. Yet despite herself, and despite the hurt he'd inflicted upon her, her ears perked up whenever there was a mention of his name. She knew he and his bride had moved to Linder Creek. She knew he worked at a company that sold tractors, and his wife was the favorite nurse at the local hospital.

But she hadn't known they were expecting a baby. Well, it was inevitable, wasn't it? It was bound to happen sooner or later. She used to brace herself for the news, but when it hadn't been forthcoming for a while, she'd put it aside. And now, here it was.

Why, oh, why hadn't he joined church before he'd left? Then no one would talk about him. She wouldn't hear his name coming from anyone's lips, for he would have been shunned and talk of him would have been forbidden.

She bit her lip and scowled at herself, putting the mirror down. What an unseemly train of thought. She should be ashamed of herself.

She sighed. At least, Robert wouldn't be at the youth singing that evening. It was only for single folks, even if they were well on in years. She remembered all the times Robert had given her a ride home from the youth sings. She would count down the days until preaching Sunday rolled around again, just so they'd have a sing, and Robert would ask to take her home.

She smiled at the memory. Of course, he never took her straight home. They went the long way—the *very* long way—to her house, laughing and chatting and enjoying each other the entire way. When he'd stop at the end of her drive, he'd put the reins in his lap and turn to her. Then he'd take her in his arms and kiss her. Her heart took flight each and every time. Of course, he didn't start kissing her until they'd been courting for months. And it wasn't long after that, when he'd proposed.

"But you haven't joined church," she'd protested, knowing they couldn't marry unless he did.

"I've been taking instruction. I only have a few weeks left, and then I'll become a member." His eyes had twinkled then, as he visualized it. "We can marry come fall."

She'd rested her head on his shoulder then. "I can't wait, Robert. Truly. It's going to be wonderful."

He'd reluctantly let her go, and she'd run into the house on wings.

And then, Robert had fallen from a stepladder and broken his arm. Of course, Old Mae, the district herbal woman, had sent him to the hospital. She didn't set broken bones; she left that to the *Englisch* doctors.

And Robert had met a nurse named Patsy. And that was the beginning of the end. Ruth would never understand how he could give her up so easily. What was it about Patsy that took him not only from her but from his Amish faith?

It didn't make sense no matter how she pondered it. And Robert hadn't enlightened her.

"I'm sorry, Ruth. Truly, I am. But it's best. Aren't you glad this didn't happen after..." He'd stopped then, his face flaming red.

"After what, Robert?" she'd cried. "After we'd married? Are you saying you would have left your *wife* for her?" She heard her voice raise until it became shrill.

"*Nee*," he countered, flustered. "That ain't what I meant. I just meant..." He stopped and sighed heavily. "I'm sorry, Ruth. But it's just the way it is."

But she couldn't let it go that easily. "You're leaving your faith?"

"Not my faith, Ruth. I still believe in *Gott*."

"But you're leaving your life here? Your Amish roots? Has she tempted you so much?" Ruth's eyes burned with tears, and her nose was running.

"Tempted? *Nee*." His expression tightened, and Ruth saw clearly he was gone from her.

She'd slumped against the side of the buggy, suddenly with no energy and nothing more to say. He'd snapped the reins, taking her back to her drive. She opened the door and nearly fell out, just managing to catch herself.

"I'm sorry, Ruth," he said again, but she was already walking away. She hadn't bothered to shut the buggy door, but she heard it shut then, magnifying inside her head into an ear-blasting slam. She'd winced and kept walking.

She shook herself from her reverie. That was over. Months and months ago. Robert had wasted no time in marrying the nurse and moving away. His actions had horrified his parents and broken the heart of his grandparents. The entire district had been teaming with gossip and speculations over the whole mess for weeks.

And Ruth had felt like a fool. A devastated fool. For weeks and weeks, she didn't show her face in public except at preaching services. And then she didn't stay for the community meal afterward. She left immediately, despite her mother's pleas for her to stay.

And she'd stopped going to youth singings, too. It was simply too much to bear.

But now, here she was getting ready for one again. About time, she supposed, considering Robert was about to become the father of another woman's baby. What had she been waiting for? Had she really put her life on hold after he'd left her?

Why? Now, as she considered the depth of it, she was shocked. Had she gotten so off track? Had she really allowed her heartbreak to keep her from living the rest of her life?

She walked to her bed and sank down on the bright blue and yellow quilt she and her mother had made three years before. Goodness, but they'd worked hard on it. It had turned out so beautifully that sometimes Ruth didn't want to use it. She used to laugh with her mother that it should be framed and hung on exhibit somewhere.

She took a slow breath, considering the last months of her life. She'd started a new business at least. She'd always enjoyed making wind chimes, but she'd never considered it more than a hobby. Until Annie's cousin wanted one and offered to pay her for it. Ruth had made her a wind chime, taking extra care to fashion a wooden cloud at the top of it. Annie's cousin had been delighted, and from that, word had spread. When Ruth found herself making wind chimes at the rate of nearly ten per month, she'd decided to open a little shop.

Her profit wasn't huge, but it was enough that someday, she might be able support herself, if she needed to. And if she could find a way to own her shop outright and not need to pay rent, her profits could easily support her. Not lavishly, but then she had no desire for lavish. She was quite content with her simple Amish life.

Unlike Robert—who had gone fancy so quickly it made heads spin.

She shuddered, blocking him from her thoughts. Interesting how she seldom thought of Matthew anymore. He was her first love. When he'd gotten cancer, the entire district had prayed for him. Ruth had been certain he would be healed. But as the weeks wore on, she'd had to face the fact he wasn't getting better. He was worsening day by day. When he passed, she'd felt empty and numb, and her faith had curled up into a useless wad of paper, tossed into a corner. It had taken a full year before she'd felt like herself again. Well, not exactly herself, but the new version of herself. But then Robert had come along, and life brightened. It was good again.

"And that was my problem," she muttered to herself. "I don't need a man to make life *gut*. I only need *Gott*."

She stood and resolutely blew out her candle. She felt her way to the door and marched down the shadowy hallway to the stairs. They were illuminated by the gas lantern her father always lit and hung near the front door.

It was nearly Christmas. Her family was safe and healthy. *She* was safe and healthy. Life was good.

Chapter Four

Twenty minutes later, Ruth climbed into Annie's buggy and settled into the leather seat.

"I'm so glad you decided to come," Annie said, grinning before turning back to concentrate on her driving.

"Me, too," Ruth said simply.

Annie gave her a quick glance. "Truly? You're happy to be going?"

"I'm happy to be going."

Annie's brow crinkled—perfectly visible with the filtered light from the street lamps. "What's happened?"

"Not a thing," Ruth said, growing confused. "Why are you asking?"

"Because you sound…" Annie hesitated, "…different."

"What do you mean by different?"

Annie hesitated again, and then she said, "You sound more normal-like than usual. Like maybe you really are happy."

"I'm happy," Ruth said, her voice questioning.

"Please don't get upset," Annie said. "It's just you haven't sounded happy for months. Since … well, since Robert left you." She sighed. "I've been worried. But tonight, I don't know. Has something happened?"

Shame flicked through Ruth, but she set it aside. There was no reason to make herself feel bad. Didn't her *mammi* always tell her, "What's passed is past." And now, God willing, she was going to take that to heart. Finally.

"I've wasted enough time feeling bad about Robert."

Annie actually laughed. "You have no idea how happy that makes me. *Ach,* Ruth, but it's nice to have you back."

Ruth smiled, feeling a bit unbalanced. Had she really been so awful? Or at least so obvious in her sadness? Goodness, but it was well beyond time to let it all go. She paused, searching herself for the accustomed dark cloud that usually hovered over her. And then she started laughing, too.

"I do feel better," she said. "I do."

"What happened?"

"I don't know." Ruth giggled. "And I'm not going to question it to death. That's what I usually do. I'm just going to enjoy it."

"Right," Annie agreed. She snapped the reins and chuckled. "It's going to be a *gut* sing tonight."

Caleb sat in the buggy, clenching the reins. He had no desire whatsoever to go to this youth singing. He especially had no desire to take Ephraim. But he had even less desire to stay home and put up with his father's judgmental glare. So, there he sat, waiting for his brother to join him in the buggy.

He was just ready to go back inside and holler for Ephraim to come when his brother bounded out of the house and down the steps. He climbed in and shut the door.

"Let's go," he said.

Caleb snapped the reins, and they started down the drive. There was a fluttering of snowflakes that evening, but they didn't look too serious. It had been snowing lightly for most of the day. Caleb guessed it was only just below freezing temperatures, and he didn't expect the snow to increase much.

"You got your eye on anyone special?" Ephraim asked, his voice normal, as if nothing had passed between them lately.

"*Nee*." Caleb's grip on the reins tightened. "You?"

Ephraim laughed. "I've got my eye on more than one..."

Of course, he did. Caleb kept quiet. Bessie plodded on, in no particular hurry to get anywhere. Caleb shifted slightly in his seat. He wanted to chat with Ephraim like he used to, but things had become so strained that his mouth simply wouldn't cooperate. Finally, he sighed and leaned into the silence.

But Ephraim wasn't having it that night. "It ain't my fault, you know."

Caleb glanced over at him, knowing immediately what he was talking about. It was true—in a way. Ephraim hadn't asked for the buggy shop. But he had been the one whose manner of living had alarmed Vernon. If he'd been more settled, more mature, more... Caleb shook his head. It was over and done now. Vernon was dead. There was no changing things.

"You can have the shop," Ephraim said. "I don't like working there. I don't like going to the same place every day and doing the same things."

"You've hardly been there," Caleb said, his voice harsher than he'd intended.

"I've been there every day since *Daadi* died. *Dat's* made sure of that."

"You come late and leave early," Caleb said. "You can't run a business like that."

"I'm there," Ephraim snapped. "I don't want to be, but I am. I'm showing up."

Caleb took a deep breath. There was so much more to running a shop than showing up. Caleb was trying; he truly was. He was trying to teach Ephraim all he needed to know and all he needed to do. But it was frustrating. Caleb just wanted to do it all himself—he enjoyed it; he'd done it for years. But he couldn't—not and honor his grandfather's wishes.

And watching Ephraim botch it or treat it lightly or ignore things altogether was more than Caleb could take. What Caleb really wanted to do was leave. It would wrench his heart to give up the shop, but it would be infinitely worse to stay around and watch Ephraim destroy it.

"Well?" Ephraim said, exasperated.

Caleb gave a start. "Well, what?"

"You resent me, don't you? All this wasn't my fault, wasn't my doing, but you blame me."

Caleb blew out his breath. Ephraim was right. "I guess so," he reluctantly agreed.

"It ain't my fault. Take the shop. I don't care."

"You have to care," Caleb told him. "That's the whole point."

"Sometimes I think *Daadi* hated me."

"*Ach*! How can you say that?"

Ephraim shook his head. "He knows I hate selling. He knows I never wanted a thing to do with that shop."

"But it will make you a *gut* living. It will support your future family. It will allow you to serve the people. It will—"

"Spare me," Ephraim burst out, holding up his hand. "I've heard it all from *Dat*. I've heard it all *a hundred times*. Why won't anyone listen to me? I don't want to do it."

Caleb blew out his breath. "We're almost there. Let's not talk about it anymore."

"Gladly," Ephraim said sharply.

Caleb turned into the Stoltzfus place and drove to the barn, joining the row of buggies already there. He pulled to a stop, reached behind himself to grab a blanket for Bessie, and then got out. Ephraim walked toward the barn without another word.

Chapter Five

"Look," Annie pointed out under her breath. "There's Ephraim Ebersole."

Ruth followed her gaze and saw the lanky young man enter the barn. He was grinning as he waved at some of his friends.

"I hear he got the buggy shop."

"What do you mean *got* it?" Ruth asked.

"His *daadi* left it to him. You knew Vernon Ebersole, didn't you? You weren't at his funeral."

Ruth sighed. Another evidence of how she'd allowed her own depression to govern what she did. No more. She would attend every funeral, every wedding, and every celebration from now on. No more of this hibernating—or whatever it was she'd been doing.

"*Ach*, there's his brother. Goodness, but he looks upset."

Again, Ruth followed Annie's gaze. Caleb Ebersole had just walked into the barn, his expression forbidding. Her brow raised as she watched him. Once someone called his name, there was a complete transformation on his face. The lines cleared and the darkness left his eyes He smiled and called back, moving toward a cluster of young men.

Ruth frowned slightly. It had been forced. His change of expression; she recognized it, having done it hundreds of times herself. Caleb Ebersole was deeply troubled by something. Either that, or deeply hurt. She found her curiosity piqued. What was it that was bothering him? She shuddered involuntarily. It was none of her business. None at all.

She was there to have an enjoyable time. Nothing more. She certainly wasn't there to stick her nose where it didn't belong.

"Come on," Annie said, snatching her hand and dragging her to where a group of young women stood. "Hey, everyone. Look who I brought with me."

Ruth smiled as everyone greeted her enthusiastically, telling her how glad they were she'd come that evening. Within minutes, they'd all found a place to sit on the female side of the barn. Ruth settled in, actually looking forward to the singing. She wondered whether they would sing any Christmas carols and found herself hoping they would. It was such a short season to enjoy the beautiful music. She particularly liked it when they sang "Silent Night" in German. The beauty of it never failed to bring tears to her eyes.

Mark Stoltzfus rose and opened the evening with silent prayer. And then he announced the first selections. Ruth grinned when he named, "Joy to the World," as the first song. She was surprised by how happy she was to be there. She nudged Annie, who sat beside her, and gave her a happy nod. Annie seemed to know what she meant and smiled back.

Mark began singing. Everyone joined in immediately, the barn rich with the sounds of the favorite Christmas carol. Tears burned in Ruth's eyes as she sang about the baby Jesus. She glanced around at those near her and saw the song meant a lot to many of them, too; she could tell by the expressions on their faces. She glanced over to the men's side of the barn and her eyes met Caleb Ebersole's. For an electrifying moment, something passed between them. She pulled her gaze away, completely unsettled. *What was that?*

She hardly knew Caleb. He'd been four years ahead of her in school, so although they were in the same place a lot, they didn't speak much. Nor did they have much to do with each other. He hung around with the students his age, just as she did. But just then, it was as if they shared something. She felt his sorrow, and perhaps it resonated with the sorrow she'd battled for so long.

His *daadi* had just died. That must be it. But it wasn't. She instinctively knew there was something more there, and a part of her wanted to reach out to him, to comfort him. She stopped singing, and her breathing turned jagged. It had been months and months since she'd felt such compassion for another person. Dearest Lord, had she been so wrapped up in herself all this time? Had she not even noticed when others were suffering?

Well, she was noticing now. It unnerved her, making her instantly restless. She wanted to get up and leave. Go home. Retreat to her room.

Annie was staring at her now, a troubled look on her face. Ruth licked her lips and opened her mouth to sing again. No sound came, but she mouthed the words. Annie's eyes narrowed, and Ruth knew she wasn't fooling her. Still, she continued. When the next verse started, she joined in for real.

This whole day had been one for revelations. And Ruth wasn't pleased with what she'd seen. Thankfully, she had agreed to come, and thankfully, there was no way she could slip away. She needed to face life again, and if that meant she would hurt for someone else's pain, then so be it. For she did hurt. The look in Caleb's eyes haunted her even though she was staring straight ahead.

During the rest of the songs, Ruth joined in, grateful she could tick through the memorized verses, but her mind was far away. More than once, she wanted to glance again to the men's side of the barn. She wanted to see if Caleb was looking her way again. But of course, she managed to keep her gaze front and center, except when Annie nudged her now and then with question marks in her eyes.

When Mark told them it was time for refreshments, Annie wasted no time. "What is going on with you, Ruth? Why were you fake singing? You were all happy, and then you weren't."

Ruth pulled Annie off to the side where no one could hear them. "I'm happy. I just... Well, I just looked at Caleb Ebersole is all."

Annie grimaced. "Huh? What do you mean?"

"He's sad, and it affected me. That's all. I'm fine now. Let's go eat." She made to walk off, but Annie grabbed her arm and pulled her back.

"Of course, he's sad. I still don't get it."

Ruth sighed. "I don't really, either. And it doesn't matter, does it? I'm fine, and I'm hungry."

Annie paused for a moment, and then she laughed. "You're right. Let's go get some popcorn. And I think I saw some doughnuts, too. I hope they're from Widow Bieler. She makes the best in the district."

"That she does," Ruth agreed with a chuckle.

The two of them wandered over to the two long tables filled with goodies. Ruth greeted more of her friends. She glanced around looking for Caleb, but she didn't see him. That was odd. Had he left? She saw Ephraim. Hadn't the brothers come together?

Unless Caleb took the buggy to give some girl a ride home. The thought niggled at her, which was absurd. Why should that bother her?

Annie was deep in a conversation about the best way to fry doughnuts, so Ruth grabbed a oatmeal raisin cookie and wandered off. She didn't want to admit to herself she was looking for Caleb, but she was. When she reached the barn door, she hesitated. She hadn't put on her coat, and it was cold outside. Besides, what could be her reason for being outside in the first place?

"*Ach*, Ruth, there you are."

Ruth sighed, putting on a pleasant expression. Peggy Lehman was ambushing her, as only Peggy could do.

"I saw you singing, but your heart didn't seem to be in it," Peggy observed, coming to stop a mere foot in front of Ruth. Ruth instinctively backed up a pace, but Peggy came forward, matching it. Ruth only managed to hold in her dread of the girl.

"I was singing," she stated.

"Oh, sure, you were to a point. How are you doing? I'm not surprised you are upset tonight."

"Who said I was upset?" Ruth asked, her voice turning sharp.

"*Ach,* now don't get upset with *me.* I can read people's expressions, Ruth. Surely, you know that. And I was reading yours loud and clear."

Ruth gave her a cool look. "Oh, were you?"

Peggy laughed and came even closer yet—so close, Ruth was surprised she didn't feel Peggy's spittle. Again, she attempted to back away, but it was no use.

"I like to watch people. I find out the most wondrous things. Well, maybe not wondrous, but interesting. Like did you know Sarah is fighting again with her father? It's as plain as day on her face. I could read it a million miles away. Now, as you can guess, Sarah—"

"Sarah is our friend," Ruth interrupted curtly, but Peggy didn't get the message.

"*Jah, jah,* of course, she is. But she's also been fighting with her father for months about this job that she wants. It's with an *Englisch—*"

"Peggy, please..."

Peggy stopped abruptly. "*Jah,* you're right. We should be talking about you... How are you, Ruth? I mean, really?"

"I'm fine."

"It's so odd that you chose this sing to make your big return—"

"This is hardly my big return," Ruth said, growing even more annoyed.

"But to come today when Robert and his wife are in town. And did you know, they're expecting? Well, of course, you know. Isn't it amazing how he can just come right home with no consequences at all? It makes a person wonder, doesn't it? I mean, truly, did he put off joining church for just such a reason? I mean, he would be shunned. Instead, he just wanders right home, bringing that nurse with him. And what of—"

"Peggy," Ruth cried. Her annoyance had faded, and now all she felt was embarrassed and sad and put out. If she wasn't careful, she would slip right back into the emotional trap she'd been wallowing in for months.

Peggy clasped her hand over her mouth. "*Ach*, I've been thoughtless. I figured you were still suffering from that whole mess. I shouldn't have mentioned it at all."

But the intense curiosity in her eyes belied her words completely. Peggy enjoyed riling people up; there were no two ways about it.

When Ruth didn't say anything, Peggy continued. "It has to be upsetting to you. And I understand your upset. All of us do."

All of us do? Had Peggy been talking about her to others? And why wouldn't she?

Ruth stepped back again. "I'll see you later, Peggy." And with that, she turned and left the barn, going out in the cold even without her coat. She figured that would give Peggy more to gossip about, but right then, all she cared about was getting away. What was wrong with Peggy anyway? That she would enjoy upsetting others so.

It took a moment for Ruth's eyes to adjust to the darkness. It was nearly complete during that time of a December evening in Indiana. But out on the road, there was a streetlamp whose light filtered onto the property. Ruth stood for a moment, breathing heavily of the night air. Suddenly, she heard something rustle behind her and realized she wasn't alone. She whirled and saw Caleb leaning against the barn wall.

"Sorry," he said. "I didn't mean to scare you."

She gave a half laugh. "You didn't. Not really."

"You don't have a coat on."

She shivered. "I know. I won't stay out here long."

"I guess you found my hiding place."

"Are you hiding?" she asked, surprised at his candor.

"In a way." She could see his smile in the dim light. He went on. "You, too? What are you hiding from?"

"I'm not hiding..." she said and then laughed. "I s'pose I am."

He laughed with her. "It's a *gut* place to hide out here, but it does help if you wear a coat."

She shook her head. "I wasn't planning on coming outside."

"So you needed a quick escape?"

She chuckled. "You're way too close to the truth."

He nodded, then, and it grew silent between them. Ruth could hear the faint night sounds of a farm, so much quieter in winter. Even a light snow covering seemed to muffle things. She shivered again, knowing she'd have to go back in right soon, but finding she didn't want to. It was comfortable to stand out there with Caleb Ebersole, even if neither of them said anything.

He moved, and she saw he was taking off his coat.

"*Nee,*" she protested, but she was too late. He was handing his coat to her. At first, she wasn't going to take it, but then, she didn't want to seem ungrateful. She took it from him, feeling its warm weight in her hands. She put it around her shoulders, smelling the outdoors on it. But there was another smell, too, leather and rubber... She thought that odd until she remembered he worked with buggies. Or used to, anyway. She wasn't sure what was happening lately at Ebersole Buggies.

"Better?" he asked.

"Much," she answered. She felt a bit guilty that he was now the one shivering, but she was surely enjoying the warmth of his coat.

The chatter and merriness from inside the barn grew louder, and Ruth feared some of the youth were ready to come outside, but the noise faded again. She wondered what it would look like if someone did come out the door and saw the two of them standing there. And then she thought of Peggy and started to laugh.

"What is it?" Caleb asked.

"I was thinking about Peggy Lehman and what she would think of us if she came outside right now."

Caleb shook his head. "I hate to think."

Ruth couldn't suppress her laughter. "I am almost tempted to lure her out here just to see…"

"You are a wicked thing, Ruth Riehl."

He was teasing, of course, but she liked hearing her full name on his lips.

"Perhaps so."

He straightened up, then, so as not to lean against the barn wall anymore. "I'm joking."

"I know."

Silence again stretched between them. She saw he was definitely shivering now. She slipped the coat from her shoulders.

"*Nee*, you can have it," he said, holding up a hand to stop her.

"I... I should be getting back inside..."

"And not give folks something to gossip about?"

"Now *you* are the wicked one, Caleb Ebersole."

He grew still, and they stared at one another. The amused look had faded from his eyes, and in its place was a sober look, a look of pondering.

"I-I ... I was joking, too," she stammered. What had happened? What had become of the light, teasing air between them?

Some indefinable emotion sparked in his eyes. She shifted her weight, suddenly feeling uneasy.

"Go on in," he said finally. "Your lips will turn blue." His gaze touched her mouth, and then he looked away. Was he dismissing her? Whatever this had been, whatever had passed between them, was clearly gone. He was back to the sad man she'd seen earlier.

She backed away, and then turned and hurried through the barn doors, the heat inside nearly making her stumble.

Chapter Six

Caleb unhitched Bessie and brushed her down. He took his time putting her in her stall. He even gave her a scoop of hay and checked her water. Often this late in the evening, he made quick work of tending to Bessie, but not tonight. He dragged it out, not ready to go inside. Ephraim had offered to help him with the buggy, but Caleb didn't want his help. He'd spent enough time with Ephraim that day.

In truth, he'd spent enough time with Ephraim to last a lifetime.

He set the pitchfork against the side of the barn near the stalls. He took down the lantern from its nail, and snuffed it out, replacing it in the dark. He stood for a moment and let his eyes adjust. Then he made his way to the barn door.

That girl... Ruth Riehl. She was a lively one. It had been forever since he'd bantered with a girl like that. He wondered if he ever had. She was quick on her feet. And she hadn't been after him, that was clear. So often, if he talked to a girl of age, he could see her assessing him as potential husband material. And then the subtle flirting would commence. He shied away from it. He didn't like being studied—he wanted to know a girl. Have a friendship with her before even thinking about courtship. But alas, girls didn't think that way. At least, the girls he knew.

But Ruth; she was different. He'd detected none of that assessment when he'd been with her. He found that he'd enjoyed being with her, too. Even when neither of them said anything, it wasn't uncomfortable. He'd been sour that evening; he should never have gone to the singing. He was pouting—something he hated. Yet, there he was. Truly, he was pathetic these days. And it tainted his grief for his grandfather, which only made it worse. For he did grieve for Vernon Ebersole. Caleb had spent nearly every day with him for years in the shop and there at home. And now, he was gone. Caleb felt his loss to the very core of his being.

But it was all jumbled and mixed in with his resentment and his frustration and his lostness. For if he didn't run Ebersole's Buggies, who was he? The job was his identity. It was who he was. And now, with Ephraim bumbling about as its head, Ebersole's Buggies wasn't what it had been. At least, not in Caleb's heart and mind.

Yet for a precious few minutes that evening when Ruth bantered with him, he'd forgotten about it. And goodness, how good that had felt. And then it had all rushed in once again, and he'd practically forced her to leave him alone.

His mind went back to her beautiful blue eyes, to her open smile, to her witty talk. Ruth Riehl. Hadn't there been a lot of gossip about her a year or two ago? He remembered folks tossing her name about with pitying looks and whispered comments. What had it been?

He never paid much attention to gossip, and he hadn't paid attention then. He and his grandfather were remodeling a portion of the buggy shop. Caleb had been consumed with the work and all the details.

What was it?

He jolted upright. *Ach,* he remembered now. It had to do with Robert Blank leaving the district. Robert and Ruth had been courting... He left...

The scant details he knew clicked into place. She'd been deserted. He couldn't remember why. He wished he knew the full story, for suddenly, it seemed important he know everything about the girl. But how could he find out? He couldn't ask his brother; he had no desire to speak with him unnecessarily. And he could hardly buzz about the district asking people for details about Ruth.

But he could ask about Robert Blank safely enough, couldn't he?

Ach, but what was the matter with him? Was he turning into a gossipy woman now? He chuckled ruefully and stepped outside the barn, pulling the door closed. He tromped through the deepening snow and into the side door of the house. He could hear Ephraim in the front room, talking with their folks. Good. They didn't even have to know Caleb had come in. Slipping off his shoes, he walked carefully to the stairway. He took the steps two at a time and went into his bedroom. He didn't bother to light the lantern. He felt around for his nightclothes and changed, climbing into bed. The cold sheets greeted him, and he stretched out, staring up at the dark ceiling.

Ruth's image floated in his mind's eye. Giving a sigh of disgust, he flopped onto his side and tried to go to sleep.

Ruth lay in bed, her eyes wide open in the dark. She was replaying her conversation with Peggy Lehman. Only in her mind, she was giving clever retorts that stopped Peggy in her tracks. In truth, Ruth's stomach was churning with anger. How dare Peggy approach her with talk about Robert. Peggy had been purposefully trying to get a reaction from her.

And it worked, too, didn't it? Ruth taunted herself. For there she was, stewing and fretting about the woman. And even worse, Peggy had noticed how upset Ruth had gotten.

Ruth sighed heavily. *Think of something else.*

Her mind immediately went to Caleb Ebersole. Now, he had been a welcome distraction. She was no closer to knowing what was troubling the man than before they'd talked, but she had certainly enjoyed their interaction. It was odd how she'd been drawn to him; how much she wanted to know what was bothering him.

She liked him. There was something of substance within him that called to her. Or maybe she just recognized the sadness in his eyes. Maybe that was all it was. Still, they'd had fun in the freezing cold. Or at least, she had.

She flopped over onto her side. Tomorrow she'd work on a new wind chime. Her bamboo selection of chimes was low, and with Christmas almost here, there were sure to be more sales. She had the supplies she needed, and she could work on them while she tended her shop; she'd done that plenty of times. Sometimes her customers stayed around to watch her work. She smiled. She should charge admission.

She closed her eyes, now content to be thinking about her wind chimes. The window rattled a bit as the wind hit it. How many of her chimes were singing right now, dispersed about the countryside. Many, she guessed. A warm sense of satisfaction filled her, and she finally drifted off to sleep.

Chapter Seven

Shannon Zook tidied the counter of the buggy shop and then wiped it down with a damp rag. She filed two receipts that either Ephraim or Caleb had set on her desk before she'd gotten in that morning. She gave a soft snort. It wouldn't have been Caleb. Caleb would have filed them himself. Ephraim had laid them there.

She paused in her tidying and considered the younger Ebersole brother. Why was he there, anyway? Oh, she knew the old man had wanted him there, but it was clear Ephraim's heart wasn't in it. She crinkled her nose. She didn't much like working for the lad; he had no idea what he was doing, and he didn't seem too concerned about it. Why the other day, she'd had to step in when he was giving a customer a bundle of misinformation. *Ach*, but the boy should learn what's what before he started spouting off about things. She'd managed to save the sale, however, and later, Caleb had thanked her for it.

And poor Caleb. Now, there was an unhappy man. He'd used to move about the shop with a bounce in his step and a look of content concentration on his face. He was so like his grandfather—loving every aspect of the business. But that Caleb had disappeared with the burial. Now, he wore a pinched face and hooded eyes. Shannon knew he tried, but he simply couldn't hide his disappointment or his anger.

She shuddered. It wasn't good to walk about with that much anger bottled up inside. She feared for Caleb. In some ways, she considered him her son, though she was fully aware he already had a perfectly capable mother. Still, she felt protective of the man as if he were her own kin.

She didn't feel a bit of that toward Ephraim. She felt guilty for it, but she was annoyed with him, and that didn't make for much warmth and affection. She supposed she shouldn't feel that way. It wasn't good to take up offense for others, either. God couldn't be pleased with her right now.

"Shannon, do you have the info on the Mast purchase from last month?" Caleb interrupted her thoughts.

She smiled at him. "Of course. Give me a minute."

Although they were allowed to use the computer for business purposes, they kept most of their information in ledgers, as had been done since day one of the business. Caleb wasn't exactly opposed to the computer, but they only used it when absolutely necessary.

She pulled out the current ledger and flipped through the pages. "Here you go. What exactly do you need?"

Caleb leaned over her and traced an imaginary line under the information with his finger. "It's all right here. Thanks, Shannon."

"Shouldn't Ephraim be—" she clamped her mouth shut. Goodness, but what was she doing?

Caleb straightened and looked at her. She nearly winced at the emotion in his eyes. "Of course, he should be following up on this. But he won't, so I will."

And with that, he walked away. She stared after him, mortified at her quick tongue. Caleb hardly needed reminding of the shortfalls of Ephraim. She sank into her chair, ashamed.

Caleb looked into the small office at the back of the shop. Ephraim was sitting in the chair he used to occupy. His brother didn't seem to be doing much other than staring into space; although, he did give a start when Caleb poked his head through.

"Oh. It's you."

"What are you doing?" Caleb asked.

"What should I be doing?" Ephraim asked, his voice tight. "I'm sure you have a list a mile long." He threw his hands wide. "We haven't had a customer yet this morning. What could there be to do?"

"We need to go over the inventory sheets," Caleb said. "I ordered more supplies for December than usual. I'd like to check the numbers."

Ephraim made a show of getting out of the chair. "Be my guest."

Caleb held his tongue and then drew in a slow breath. "You need to know how to do this, Ephraim. We can go over things together. This will also help you know how much to order next time. There are certain things we have to keep in stock. People are counting on us."

"I know that, brother. People are counting on *you*." He craned his neck to see out to the showroom, and his gaze stopped at Shannon, where she sat at the counter with her back facing them. "I'm sure Shannon would have plenty to say about things—and about how I'm not measuring up."

Caleb sighed. He didn't want to have this conversation again. It only stirred things up, and in truth, he didn't know how much more he could take.

"Let's not go there, all right? How about I just show you the inventory sheets and where each item is located, and how to count—"

"Truly?" Ephraim cried. "I know how to count, Caleb. I went to school just like you did."

"That's not what I meant."

"*Ach*, don't fret. I know exactly what you meant." Ephraim began pacing the small space. He ran his hand through his hair, causing it to stick up in spikes. "Why don't you pretend like I'm not here? Just go about your business."

"Because that's not what *Daadi* wanted."

Ephraim stopped pacing and stepped to Caleb until they were face to face. "*Daadi* is dead and gone. He'll never know the difference."

Caleb sucked in his breath. This was a new low, even for Ephraim. "How can you say such a thing."

Ephraim had the grace to look embarrassed, but it disappeared from his face almost immediately. "Because it's true. This is a huge failure. I don't want to be here, and you don't want me here. I'm not cut out for this—"

"How do you know?" Caleb was quick to ask. "You haven't tried."

"I don't want to try. I already know I don't want to work here. I think this experiment has gone on long enough..."

"Experiment?"

Ephraim stopped moving, and Caleb became aware of his brother's uneven breathing as it filled the small space around them. It dawned on him that this truly was as hard on Ephraim as it was on him. Maybe there was a way out. Maybe they could revisit the whole thing with their father.

Ephraim shook his head. "I'll be back later," he said curtly and left the room.

Caleb followed him, but Ephraim was too fast and was out the front door before Caleb could call him back. He stopped and leaned against the new pony cart waiting to be picked by the Schwartz family. Where was Ephraim going, anyway?

"Anywhere but here," he muttered under his breath. "Anywhere but here."

Chapter Eight

Ruth searched every supply drawer in her shop. How in the world had she gotten so low on twine? She was certain she had another roll of the hemp twine ready for the bamboo pieces she'd already cut, but it was nowhere to be seen. She sighed. Now she'd have to go into town for more. True, it was a short walk from her shop, but still she'd have to close the shop while she went. She peered through the window at the light snow falling lazily to the ground. It was sticking, but at such a slow rate, it wouldn't amount to much. She pulled on her winter coat and wrapped her scarf around her neck. She had worn her heavy black boots that day like she often did in the winter, not even taking them off while she was managing her shop.

She flipped the *Open* sign to *Closed* and stepped out onto the sidewalk. She was usually quite happy to walk the few blocks to the Arts & Crafts supply store, but today she was hoping to have a lot of customers and closing the shop for even a half hour wasn't the way to get them. She hurried her steps, and hearing something she thought might be a kitty, she wasn't looking where she was going. With a smack, she plowed into someone's back.

"*Ach*, I'm sorry!" she cried.

The someone turned and she sucked in her breath.

"Robert..."

He looked disturbed to see her, and then he gave her a bright smile, which she could tell was forced. "Why, Ruth... Hello."

"Hello." She wanted to scurry on by, but she knew that was impossible. How would it look? And she hardly wanted Robert to think she was still pining after him.

He glanced around as if checking to see whether others were noting this awkward reunion. "How are you?"

"Fine." And then she made herself add, "And you?"

"I'm... We're... Well, I s'pose you'll hear it soon enough. We're going to have a baby."

She was distracted by his *Englisch* attire. He had on jeans and a leather jacket—or what she supposed was leather, a stocking cap, and he was clean-shaven, no beard. But what had she expected? He'd left the Amish church for that nurse, hadn't he? He would hardly still be dressing as an Amish man. But seeing him this way, unnerved her. Like she knew him but didn't know him.

Which she supposed was true enough.

"I-I heard," she managed to say, coming back to his comment. "Congratulations."

His face flushed. "Thanks. And you?"

And me, what? she wondered. Was he trying to find out if she was married? If she was pregnant, too? Well, he had eyes in his face, didn't he? She was clearly not pregnant. Besides, knowing the Amish grapevine, he would already know the answer to both those questions.

His face turned a darker shade of red as he clearly realized the same thing she was thinking.

"I... I better get going," he said clumsily.

"*Jah*, you better." She blinked at her own words. Had she sounded as rude as she thought?

"You can ... tell your folks hello for me."

Why would she do that? She didn't want to even bring up his name. But she smiled—or at least, she hoped it was a smile, and nodded.

He turned to go and then turned back to her. She held her breath. What now?

"Ruth?"

"Jah?"

"I'm sorry it all turned out this way for you. I-I was ... cruel, I think."

Her eyes widened. Was he apologizing? At long last? She could hardly believe her ears. She was so stunned that her knees went wobbly, and she nearly faltered right there on the sidewalk.

"I've surprised you," he said.

"J-jah."

"I am sorry, Ruth. I've been wanting to tell you that for some time, now. I hope you can forgive me."

She blinked, feeling sudden tears prick the backs of her eyes. "I..." Her words seemed stuck in her throat. She swallowed hard, past the growing lump. *"Jah.* Of course."

She hoped she meant it. Indeed, she hoped she had forgiven him a long time ago, but in truth, she wasn't sure she had. Maybe with his apology, she could truly put Robert out of her mind and heart forever.

He exhaled with relief. "Thank you."

She wanted to go now. Surely, there was nothing more to say, and she felt awkward standing with him on the street where anyone could see them. She was just ready to say good-bye when Peggy Lehman burst out of the butcher shop. Her eyes bulged with delighted surprise when she caught sight of them.

She bustled right over.

"Why Robert Black, imagine you back in town."

Ruth saw Robert's grimace, even though he clearly tried to hide it. He faced Peggy with a sigh. "Hello, Peggy, how are you?"

"Me? *Ach,* I'm right fine. Fit as a fiddle, as the *Englischers* say. How are you? And how's your wife?" Peggy's head swiveled this way and that. "Where *is* your wife?"

Robert's face looked pinched. "She's not with me right now."

Ruth noted he hadn't answered Peggy's question, and she couldn't help but smile. Robert was certainly more clever than she in how to handle Peggy's intrusions and meddling.

"And here you are with Ruth. Talking about old times, I imagine."

"*Nee,*" Ruth interjected quickly. "We're talking about the weather. It isn't too bad considering how close we are to Christmas, don't you think, Peggy?"

Robert shot Ruth an amused look, and for a split second, time rolled back, and they were together again—in on a private joke. Ruth's mouth went dry, but she managed to hold her expression.

"Well, I... The weather? *Jah,* I s'pose it's not too cold," Peggy stammered. But she didn't falter for long. Her sharp eye focused back on Robert. "So, your wife is at your family's place?"

So. She wasn't going to give up.

"I'll give her your greetings," Robert said smoothly.

Peggy frowned. "*Jah*. Do that." Her gaze flitted back and forth from Robert to Ruth. "Well," and here she drew herself up to her full height—which wasn't too impressive—but somehow her presence puffed up and filled the space anyway as if she were a good foot taller than she was, "I s'pose I'd better be going."

She paused a moment more, as if trying to figure out how she could dredge up some gossipy tidbits with such unwilling targets. And then, with a deeper frown, she bustled away.

Both Ruth and Robert were silent for a good thirty seconds, and then they began to laugh. Ruth covered her mouth, not wanting the sound to carry, but Robert clearly didn't care. His laugh was loud and hearty. Soon, they were both breathless and they grew quiet once more.

And then Robert said, "*Ach,* but that felt *gut* to laugh."

Hearing him slip back into his Amish accent caused Ruth's heart to lurch, but she quickly realized it meant nothing. How could it?

"Thank you, Ruth," he said. "It was nice to see you and to talk to you." He pursed his lips and gave her a look full of gratitude. "And thank you. Thank you again for forgiving me."

"It's in the past," she said quietly, knowing more than ever before the truth of her words. He touched her arm softly and then turned and walked away. She watched him go and was both surprised and relieved to feel no emotional wrench. She smiled and then, inexplicably, her mind filled with the image of Caleb Ebersole.

Chapter Nine

Ephraim didn't return to the buggy shop that day. Caleb carried on as usual, but he was distracted. This simply wasn't working. He needed to have a talk with his father about it, which he dreaded. For some reason, his father was being completely unreasonable. Was it because he was trying to placate Caleb's mother? Vernon had been her father, after all. She was devastated by his loss, and maybe his dad was trying to comfort her, or keep him alive somehow, by following his wishes.

Caleb hated to admit it, but Ephraim was right. Vernon Ebersole was dead and gone and would never know if Ephraim took over the shop or not. Caleb wouldn't have stated it in quite the harsh way Ephraim had, but the truth of it was hard to ignore.

Caleb couldn't accept the idea that he had to spend the rest of his working life here at the shop, dealing with Ephraim every day. Not that he didn't love his brother; he did. But his behavior here was too much to ignore and too much to bear. Not to mention the fact that the shop wouldn't survive Ephraim's leadership, and Caleb couldn't bear to watch it falter and fail.

But if Caleb didn't work here, where would he work? For the hundredth time since his grandfather had died, Caleb tried to figure out what he would do.

He couldn't. Because he only wanted to work with buggies and the customers and the million other things that running a shop entailed.

Yet ... he could start his own shop. He paused as the very idea grabbed his heart. He could do it, too; he had all the knowledge and experience he needed. He couldn't do it there in Hollybrook, of course. He would never put himself in competition with Ebersole's Buggies. But he could go elsewhere. He could do some research and find a nice town with a lot of Amish folk that didn't have a buggy shop.

He breathed out as excitement filled him. Yes, that was what he could do. It would be hard going at first, as he established himself. But it wouldn't take long to build his reputation. And he had some money to start out. Not enough, surely, but sufficient to rent a place and begin building his inventory. He could get a loan for the rest. He knew he could. He had a solid reputation, and the banker in town knew his family. Not that he would get a loan here, but bankers talked amongst themselves, didn't they?

His pulse raced as the exciting implications of it filled him. He hadn't felt this good, this hopeful, since Vernon spoke with him on his deathbed. Oh, Caleb wouldn't leave right away. He'd continue to show Ephraim the business, but then he'd be done. He couldn't control what Ephraim did—that was already completely obvious. But he would have fulfilled his grandfather's request even though he had never promised to do so.

Move away from Hollybrook. He'd never considered it in his life, but he sure was considering it now. The idea sparked fire in him, and he wanted to begin looking into it right away. Linder Creek, the closest Amish settlement to Hollybrook didn't have a buggy shop, but those folks came here, so he wouldn't settle there. There were a few more Amish settlements further north, some of considerable size. He knew of the few buggy shops there, and he was quite certain that Baker's Corner didn't have one.

But then, why would he limit himself to Indiana? Maybe there was a better place in Ohio or Illinois. He rubbed his hands together, the idea growing stronger and stronger. He could do this; he was certain he could.

He drew in a sharp breath. How could he tell his mother? Or his father that he was leaving to open a buggy shop elsewhere?

He'd just tell them, though not yet. He needed to develop his idea into a real plan. His heart raced, and he found himself grinning with happiness.

"*Ach,* what's got you smiling like a lad with a fish on his pole?" asked Shannon, approaching him from the bathroom. She straightened her apron a bit and tilted her head, clearly waiting for an answer.

"Shannon, you wouldn't believe it if I told you," he said happily. But he wasn't ready to divulge his secret yet. No, not yet.

Shannon shrugged and went back to the counter and wriggled onto the stool. Caleb walked across the show room into the small office. It was nearly time to close for the day. He straightened a few things that needed tidying and then glanced around the room. He'd spent days and days of his life in this room. How odd it would be to do the same work elsewhere.

He laughed. He would start outlining his plan that evening at home in his room. He'd write down everything that needed to be done; the list would be long. He didn't care. He was up for it. He laughed again, and this time, his mind flashed to Ruth Riehl. Now why in the world had she come to mind?

Because she would laugh with excitement for him. He suddenly knew this to be true. Maybe, she'd be one of the first people he'd tell. He quite liked the idea.

Ruth needed construction paper to make Christmas cards for her family and friends. They rarely exchanged gifts, but they did exchange cards. Over the years, Ruth's cards became fancier and more intricate as she experimented with cut-outs and folding the paper to make pop-ups in the middle of the cards. The Christmas before, she'd perfected a way to make a manger scene that expanded when the card was opened. It had taken her hours for each card, but she found that she enjoyed the challenge of it. She had some new ideas for this year's cards. In truth, she should have started well before now, yet she still had time.

And she didn't have to make every card so fancy.

Humming to herself, she walked down the sidewalk on the main street. She loved Christmas time. Whereas her father didn't allow many decorations in their home, the stores along the street were lavish with decorations. She slowed her walk, taking them all in. She loved the twinkle lights in red and green. Once, she'd seen a house with only blue lights hung on all the eaves and thought it staggeringly beautiful. She didn't care for the Santas, feeling they had no place during Christmas, but the trees and the winter scenes and the occasional manger were lovely.

Ahead, outside the dollar store where she'd buy her supplies, she saw Ephraim Ebersole lingering as if he weren't sure where he was going. Being younger than Caleb, Ephraim had been only a year ahead of her, and so they'd spent more time in school together. He was a mischievous student if she remembered correctly, but he'd kept the students laughing more than once.

He didn't look amused now, however. He looked troubled.

"Hello, Ephraim," she said as she neared him.

He blinked as if surprised to see her. "*Ach*, Ruth... How are you?" His brown eyes were lighter than his brother's, as was his hair, which stuck out slightly from beneath his felt hat.

"I'm fine. And you?"

He gave a huge sigh and scowled. "Fine. Why wouldn't I be? I've just gotten a whole new life."

He didn't sound fine. In truth, he sounded anything but fine.

"A whole new life?" she questioned him.

"*Jah*. Surely, you've heard. I'm now in charge of Ebersole's Buggies." He stared at her as if daring her to respond.

Her brow creased. He was acting right odd. "Um... I heard something about it, but I didn't know. Not really. So, you're the manager now? Or your *groosdaadi* gave the shop to you?"

This was news. Suddenly, a lot clicked into place. Caleb's surly mood. His negative disposition. What in the world had happened that Vernon Ebersole hadn't given the shop to Caleb? Hadn't Caleb been the brother who'd worked there for years? Not that Ruth frequented the shop, but when she had gone by on rare occasions, she couldn't remember one time when Ephraim had been there.

"You think he was a fool, don't you?" Ephraim said, his voice laced with bitterness. "I know everyone is thinking that."

"I-I..." She paused. "Why would I think that?" Her happy mood of a few moments ago plummeted. Goodness, but both the brothers dampened the Christmas spirit. But then, they'd lost their grandfather, so some upset was to be expected.

"Everyone does," Ephraim interrupted her thoughts. He flung out his hands. "The whole world."

Her eyes widened, and suddenly what he said seemed so absurd, she couldn't help but laugh. And then she clapped her hand over her mouth. She feared she'd made him angry, but instead, he started to laugh with her.

"The whole w-world..." he stammered out between laughs. "Imagine the whole world caring!" And he burst into more laughter.

She laughed right along with him. He was mimicking himself now, flinging out his arms again to encompass the whole world. When they finally stopped laughing, he looked at her, his expression now soft.

"Thank you, Ruth. I needed that laugh."

"You're the one who was funny," she responded. "You always were funny. I remember that."

He screwed up his face. "Was I?" He nodded. "I s'pose I was. Hmm. I kind of forgot. I haven't laughed much lately, and that's my fault."

The mood had lightened, and Ruth found herself enjoying their interaction.

"And what brings you downtown?" he asked. He peered behind her. "Shouldn't you be at your shop?"

She smiled. "I'm just picking up some art supplies, then I'm heading back."

"I've only been in your shop once," he told her. "You wouldn't remember that, though. I know you have lots of customers because I hear your wind chimes when I'm out and about."

"Do you?"

He smiled. "I do. Maybe one of these days, I'll come in again. I could buy one of your chimes for my family."

"Hopefully, they'd like that."

"I'm sure they would."

They fell silent then and Ephraim seemed to once again be in deep thought. And then he said, "Do you like running your shop?"

"*Jah*. I like it. I enjoy making the chimes, and hopefully, I make people happy when they buy them."

"People don't buy buggies to be happy. They buy them because they need them."

"Still, wouldn't that make them happy?"

He shrugged. "I s'pose."

"You don't like the business?" For it was clear, he was hesitant about the whole thing.

"*Nee*. I don't."

This surprised her. Ebersole's Buggies was a well-established business in town. She would think anyone would be happy to be involved. And to be in charge of it—why, that would be a wonderful thing.

Ach, Ephraim's thinking on it would be like salt in a wound to Caleb. No wonder...

"What are you thinking?" Ephraim asked her. "You look lost in thought."

She smiled. "I'm thinking that Ebersole's Buggies is a wonderful business."

"It is that." Ephraim sighed. "I should be jumping for joy at the chance. I should." He shrugged again.

"I guess we can't always control what we do or don't like."

He grinned then, as if relieved. "That's it. But some folks don't see it that way." His eyes narrowed slightly as if studying her. "Do you want to go riding with me this evening? I can get the buggy, and I don't think any more snow is expected."

Ruth was taken aback, not expecting an invitation. Caleb's face filled her mind, though she couldn't think why. It wasn't him doing the asking. She'd never been particularly impressed with Ephraim, but chatting with him had been nice, and there was no reason to turn him down. She hadn't gone riding with anyone since Robert, and goodness, wasn't it time to do so? Was Robert's rejection really the end of her romantic life?

"All right," she said.

He perked up. "Really? *Ach,* but that's *gut.* I'll come by around seven. Will that suit?"

"It'll suit right fine. I'll meet you at the end of the drive."

Ephraim grinned. "This started out as a bad day, but it suddenly got a whole lot better." He tipped his head at her and then turned and walked away.

She took a deep breath and hoped she'd done the right thing. *Goodness, but why do you have to analyze everything so?* she asked herself. *Can't you just enjoy yourself?*

But as she went into the dollar store, her thoughts once again shifted to Caleb, and for a quick unreasonable moment, she felt as if she were betraying him somehow.

Chapter Ten

Caleb froze and stood unmoving, staring at the scene across the street and down a ways. The cold air nipped his face and ears, but he hardly noticed. His stomach was tight, and his hands curled into fists. Was that Ephraim? Standing there talking to Ruth?

The very same Ruth who had been filling his thoughts since the youth sing? The very same Ruth whose quick wit and sweet smile had charmed him enough to pull him out of his bad humor?

How was it possible that his brother was talking to her? Caleb kept watching, his feet cemented to the sidewalk and his breathing gone shallow. Was Ruth nodding now? What was she agreeing to? Surely, Ephraim wasn't pursuing her, was he?

And what was Ephraim doing standing out there on the sidewalk anyway? Caleb had wondered where he was—thinking he'd escaped to Linder Creek or something. He surely hadn't thought he was just wandering around town, doing anything possible to shirk his responsibilities.

Ephraim was walking away now, and Ruth was turning to go into the dollar store. If he hurried, he could "accidentally" run into her there. He began to move then, heading across the street, when he stopped himself. He stepped back onto the curb. What was he thinking? Why should he go chasing after Ruth?

Because you like her, came the answer, ringing through his mind.

And Ephraim clearly liked her, too. If Caleb didn't get a move on, Ephraim would steal Ruth right from under his nose. He balanced there on the curb, trying to decide what to do, and then he moved again, crossing the street with intent. He walked through the door of the dollar store and heard the tinkle of the bell, announcing his entrance. He easily spotted Ruth, in the aisle where there were school and office supplies. She was bending over, studying packages of construction paper.

"Hello, Ruth."

She looked up, surprised. And then she did a double-take and stood. "Goodness, but I've just seen Ephraim. How odd to run into you both one right after the other."

"Oh?" he said, acting as if he didn't know. "I s'pose that is odd."

She stood there smiling and looking at him, and he suddenly couldn't think of anything to say. Goodness, but he might have planned this out better.

The silence stretched and she began to fidget. He could see her trying to think of something to say, too. They both opened their mouths at the same time, but his words came first.

"Would you like to go riding with me sometime? Maybe this evening?"

Her stricken look cut into him. *Ach,* was it such an unpleasant prospect? Spending time with him? He gulped, wondering how he could take it back.

"I-I..." she stammered.

"Never mind," he interrupted her. "Let's pretend I never asked."

"But you did ask," she said, her forehead creasing.

"It's clear you don't want to go. Never mind."

She looked annoyed now. "Don't assume you know what I'm thinking," she snapped. "You don't know at all."

That brought him up short. He faltered for a moment, regretting the whole thing. Regretting he'd come across the street in the first place. But he was there now. "So, tell me what you're thinking," he said.

"I'm thinking I already have an engagement for this evening." She raised her chin.

And then it dawned on him, becoming painfully clear. Ephraim had beat him to it. He blew out his breath. Was this the way it was to be from then on? Ephraim beating him to everything he wanted? Caleb was suddenly more than glad he had a plan forming for his future. He wouldn't have to deal with Ephraim at all when he moved away and started his own shop.

"Are you all right?" she asked, looking concerned now instead of irritated.

"Of course, I'm all right."

When he didn't speak further, she asked, "Aren't you going to ask me for another night?"

He blinked. "Do you want me to?"

She scowled. "Do you make it this hard for every girl you ask to go riding?"

"I don't ask girls to go riding." His eyes bulged. Did he have to reveal everything to Ruth Riehl? He felt his cheeks go hot.

"You don't?" Now, she looked mischievous, as if she were enjoying his misery. "Then I am most honored, *ain't so?*" She widened her eyes in playful innocence.

He shook his head but then couldn't help but laugh. "*Ach*, but you are a difficult one, Ruth."

"Am I? So is that why you're not asking me for another evening?"

"I'm getting to it," he countered, then looked around hoping no one was near enough to hear him. No one was. "Would you like to go out riding with me another evening?"

She tilted her head, as if considering. "Hmm. When exactly?"

"Tomorrow night."

She continued to ponder, sighing with exaggerated concentration. Then, she straightened. "I do believe I would, Caleb Ebersole."

He felt a rush of pleasure at her words. "All right. Will seven o'clock suit?"

She nodded. "It'll suit."

"*Gut*." He said, and without another word, he turned on his heels and practically ran from the store. He felt like an absolute fool.

But he had to admit, he hadn't felt this pleased for a very long time.

Ruth shook her head and clasped the package of construction paper to her chest. She had a date with both Ebersole brothers one after another. She certainly hadn't expected to jump back into dating with such speed. It made her feel unbalanced somehow, but she scolded herself, telling herself it was about time. And so what if she dated both brothers? She had no commitment to either of them.

She bent down and picked up a bottle of glitter. Truth be told, she wasn't sure how she felt about the upcoming evenings. She almost wished she hadn't told Ephraim she'd go. At that point, she would rather be with Caleb. Yet, Ephraim was nice, and a person never really knew how things might develop. And Ephraim might even grow to love running Ebersole's Buggies. He could surprise the whole town.

Ach, that wasn't even her business, but she couldn't help her mind going that direction. If they did start actually courting, she'd hoped for someone stable, dependable. She had no interest in having her heart broken again. How many times could a person bounce back?

Numerous times, she thought. Besides, she was bordering on feeling sorry for herself, and she'd had enough of that to last a lifetime. She paused to grab some colorful markers, another bottle of glitter, and she went up to the checkout counter.

Chapter Eleven

That evening, Ruth changed her dress and put on a fresh *kapp*. She went downstairs and found her folks in the front room— her mother was embroidering by lantern light, and her father was snoozing with an open book on his chest.

"*Ach*, there you are..." Her mother's gaze narrowed. "Did you change your dress?"

"I did. I'm going out for a while."

Her mother gave a sharp intake of breath. "Are you now?"

"*Jah*. I'll see you later." Ruth nearly scurried from the room, not wanting to answer any more questions. She doubted her mother would ask many, for dating wasn't really discussed, but she knew that after all this time, her mother might not be able to hold back.

And Ruth wasn't of a mind to talk about it.

She went to the washroom and pulled on her heavy coat. She slipped into her boots and wound a scarf around her neck. She noted the small pile of evergreen boughs resting on the bench. Her father allowed the boughs to be set out as Christmas decorations, but not too many. Her mother had set out more than he liked and had to gather a few of them back and set them aside. Ruth paused a moment to inhale their pine scent. The smell always put her in the mood for Christmas—all the special food and family gatherings and the annual Christmas program at the school. In truth, there was nothing not to like about Christmas.

And bigger sales, she couldn't help but think as she went through the side door. She'd had a very good afternoon at the shop, selling four wind chimes, two of them her most expensive. She'd need to get busy and make a few more which she was sure she could do before Christmas arrived.

The air was surprisingly balmy as she hurried down the drive. She gave a small laugh. One never knew what the Indiana weather would bring. She remembered one Christmas that was so warm, folks were going about without coats on. This evening she still needed her coat, though, but the scarf wasn't necessary. She unwound it as she walked, looping it over her arm.

When she got to the end of the drive, Ephraim wasn't there. She peered down the road and didn't see a buggy coming. She had understood correctly, hadn't she? When she'd gone to tell her mother she was leaving, it had been a minute or two before seven. So, it had to be a few minutes after by now. She walked to the side of the drive and stood under a small maple tree to wait.

A car zipped by, and she idly wondered where they were going in such a rush. It seemed like cars were always going so fast. Did the *Englisch* world really move at such a speed all the time? She couldn't imagine such a thing; she was perfectly content to go at a horse's speed. There was a streetlight down the way, so she wasn't standing in the pitch dark, but it was dark enough to wonder what all was around her. She didn't particularly like standing out there alone like that.

After about ten minutes, she wondered if she'd been mistaken. Ephraim should have been there by now. He knew where she lived and would know how long it took his horse to get there. She leaned against the trunk of the tree and then thought better of it. She didn't want to get her coat dirty. She could use the time to pray, couldn't she?

"Thank you, *Gott*, for all you've given us. For your love. For your peace. For your guidance..." she paused, thinking she heard something. She stepped out from under the tree and looked well down the road again.

Nothing.

She wasn't in the mood to keep praying—she wondered what that said about her but decided not to ponder it too closely.

"Come on, Ephraim," she whispered. And then she said more loudly, "Why am I whispering? There isn't anyone to hear me."

She was tapping her toe now. She decided to sing her favorite Christmas carol. She started right in with, "Silent Night, Holy Night, all is calm…"

Was that a horse coming? She went still, but again, didn't hear anything. She resumed singing, this time more quietly so she could hear a buggy coming. She was starting the third verse when she finally did hear the distinct clip clop of a horse.

Finally, she thought. She stepped closer to the road so Ephraim would see her. When the approaching buggy didn't slow, she quickly stepped back in the shadows, watching it go by.

Not Ephraim. She was becoming annoyed now. Where was he? In all fairness, he might have had something unexpected come up. It wasn't like he could call and tell her. But still, she found herself annoyed. She might as well go back inside. What was she going to tell her mother? How embarrassing was this? And her mother wouldn't let it go, for sure and for certain. She'd question her until Ruth admitted it was Ephraim who was supposed to come.

She turned to walk back up the drive when she again heard the clip clop of a horse. Was that him? She was tempted to leave anyway, but she didn't want to be petty. She stepped back to the end of the drive, and this time the buggy slowed, coming to a stop in front of her. Ephraim leaned over and opened her door.

"Hello, Ruth."

"Hello," she answered and went over and climbed inside.

"How was your afternoon?" he asked.

Her brow furrowed. Wasn't he going to apologize for being late? "It was fine."

"*Gut*. I thought we might drive to Edmund's Pond. It's warm tonight. We could even go for a walk."

"All right." She did have her boots on, and a walk would be pleasant.

"My *mamm* made apple pie for supper, and I had an extra piece before I came. She outdid herself this time." He chuckled.

Ruth looked at him. "So that's why you were late," she asked before she could stop herself.

He gazed at her, and she could see from the streetlight coming into the buggy that he was surprised. "Late? Was I late?"

"Some."

"Sorry about that." He laughed. "*Jah*, maybe I was late at that. I did notice the time going quick like."

"How was your afternoon?" she asked, wanting to change the subject.

He shrugged. "Okay, I s'pose."

"How was the shop? Any sales?" She enjoyed talking about business, feeling grateful to be involved in it herself.

"Don't rightly know."

"You didn't work today?" Again, she spoke without thinking first.

"I told you, Ruth. I don't like the place."

"I'm sorry." She shouldn't have asked. *Ach,* she knew full well he didn't like his enforced position; hadn't he told her so that very day?

"No need to be sorry."

"So, how was your afternoon then?"

"Boring. Nothing much to do."

She wanted to question him further, but she didn't. She needed to think of something else to talk about.

"Um, are you looking forward to Christmas?"

He smiled now, and she could feel his good humor return. "I am. *Mamm* makes a wonderful pumpkin pie, and her turkey gravy is the best in the county, I'm thinking."

Ruth laughed. "My *mamm* makes *gut* gravy, too. Do you have a lot of family come over?"

He shrugged. "A fair amount, I s'pose. Although, our family ain't one of the real big ones around here." He snapped the reins. "Some families get so big, I don't rightly know how the parents support them all."

"Yet each child is a gift from *Gott*." Ruth firmly believed this, even when things got inconvenient. She was suddenly reminded she didn't have any children of her own, whereas many of her friends were married and already either had a child or two or were expecting. She braced herself against the feeling of longing that always accompanied the thought.

If only Robert hadn't... She stiffened. *Nee.*

Robert wasn't the right one for her. She glanced at Ephraim out of the corner of her eye. Neither was he. She felt it down to her bones. So why was she riding out with him? *Because he asked*, she told herself with some mortification. She should have said no. But then, he had been charming. Yet now, she saw clearly that he was quite different from what she was looking for in a beau.

Was Caleb more to her liking?

Inwardly, she cringed. She couldn't be out with one brother, thinking about the other. Her dating skills were dreadful. She nearly laughed out loud at the thought.

"What's so funny?" he asked her.

"What do you mean? Did I laugh?"

"*Nee*, you didn't. But even in the near dark, I can see you want to." His voice was light, amused.

"Nothing," she said, wondering at herself. What else would she give away by her expression?

"Do you ice skate?" he asked, abruptly changing the subject.

She smiled. "Sometimes, when Edmund's Pond freezes over."

They were pulling into the wide parking spot beside Edmund's Pond that very minute.

"Shall we go test the ice? See if it's ready."

"*Ach*, Ephraim! It won't be ready. It hasn't been freezing nearly hard enough."

He pulled the buggy to a stop and secured the reins. "Let's go see who's right."

He jumped out of the buggy and ran around to her side to open the door. She was already halfway out.

"Don't walk out on it," she cried, alarmed. For Ephraim seemed like the type to do so without a thought to his own safety. Edmund's Pond wasn't huge, but it was good-sized and quite deep in places.

He grabbed her hand and pulled her to the edge.

"Hmm," he said, observing. The light of the moon reflected off the surface of the pond. It looked frozen, but to Ruth's eyes, the ice didn't look even an inch thick.

"It's thin," Ruth said. She bent down and found a stone. She threw it onto the pond, and it skidded across the ice.

"Did you see that?" Ephraim said, laughing now. "It's thicker than you think."

Ruth rummaged around on the ground until she found a bigger stone. She hefted it back and threw it. It landed on the ice, sent out a loud crack and splash and disappeared into the depths.

He took her hand again, and he squeezed it. "You've saved me from a watery death," he said, putting on a solemn tone. "I am forever in your debt."

She pulled her hand free and fisted it on her hip. "You're awful, Ephraim Ebersole."

"That I am. Everyone would agree." He laughed again. "Still, thank you for your concern. It was touching."

She gave him a sideways look, teasing him. "You knew all the time the ice wasn't thick enough."

He cocked his head. "Maybe."

"You were just trying to get me to fret."

"Maybe."

She lightly punched his arm. "You're awful."

He shrugged. He was silent for a moment, and then he started walking on the path around the lake. "Coming?" he asked over his shoulder.

She scurried and caught up with him. Now, that she'd decided he wasn't the one for her, she relaxed and enjoyed their walk. He chatted on about how he'd gone to the movies when he was on *rumspringa*, and how he wouldn't mind going again.

"I've never been," Ruth told him.

"Not even when you were enjoying *rumspringa*?" he asked. "What *did* you do?"

"Nothing, really. I was content to stay home and go about my life." She didn't want to talk about how she'd been engaged to Matthew during that time. About how he'd grown ill with leukemia and how quickly he'd gone downhill. About how she'd helped his mother nurse him and how she and his mother had watched Matthew decline and fade away until there was nothing left of him but a hollow shell. About how he'd died and broken her heart into a million pieces.

"You didn't do anything?" There was incredulity in his tone.

Now, it was her turn to shrug.

"Would you go to the movies with me now, then? Just once? We could sneak away to Linder Creek or something. No one would see us."

She blinked at him. "B-but it's not to be done. I can't do that."

"Why not? You should have the experience at least once in your life."

She wanted to cry, *why?* There were many experiences she didn't need to have at all in her life. Besides, she had no interest in the *Englisch* movies.

"I'm still turning you down," she said.

This seemed to put him off, and she felt a subtle shift in his mood. He chatted a bit more about mundane things like crops and goats and work horses, even though she could tell he had no interest in any of it. By the time they circled back around to the buggy, she was more than ready to go home.

He evidently felt the same way. He didn't ask if she wanted to drive further than evening; he simply turned the buggy toward her home and snapped the reins. When they arrived at her drive, he leaned over her and opened the door for her.

"Thank you for coming, Ruth," he said simply.

"Thank you for asking me," she replied. She slipped out of the buggy and waved. He didn't ask if she'd like to go out riding with him again, which suited her as she would have turned him down this time. She walked slowly up her drive, enjoying the stillness of the night.

Maybe, come January, Edmund's Pond would be frozen solid enough to ice skate. She hoped so, for it was fun. She wanted to go—but not with Ephraim.

Right then, her mind went to Caleb Ebersole. She could see him flying across the ice with his hand outstretched toward her. She was just visualizing grabbing his hand when she reached the side door. Instead of Caleb's hand, she reached for the doorknob and let herself quietly into the washroom.

Chapter Twelve

Caleb had gone to the window at least twenty times that evening, peering outside into the starry night, waiting for Ephraim to return. He knew his brother was with Ruth, and it grated. When was he going to get home, anyway?

"Something bothering you, son?" his father finally asked.

So many things, Caleb wanted to answer. Instead, he said, "*Nee.* Nothing."

"You're going back and forth to that window like a yo-yo."

Caleb raised his brow at his father's comparison. He wasn't aware his father even knew what a yo-yo was. Still, he had a point. Of course, Caleb was going to raise comments with the way he'd been keeping watch through the window.

"Are you waiting for your brother?" his mother asked, looking up from the puzzle she was putting together.

"Just restless, I guess," Caleb said by way of excuse.

"If you need something to do, you could go out to the barn and reorganize those hand tools your brother messed up a month ago."

"*Gut* idea," Caleb said. He had no interest in organizing tools, but he also had no interest in hanging around and being questioned. In truth, he was annoyed with himself for his preoccupation with Ephraim's activities that evening. He went to the washroom and pulled on his heavy coat. He laced up his boots, grabbed a lit lantern, and went out to the barn. He'd no sooner walked inside, but he heard Ephraim return. He walked back outside, holding the lantern high.

Ephraim guided Bessie up to the barn door, stopped, and got out. "What are you doing out here?" he asked.

"I was going to work on the tools."

"This hour of the night?" Ephraim asked. "What are you really doing?"

"Organizing the tools."

Ephraim gave a low whistle. "You're an odd one, brother, for sure and for certain."

"And you?" Caleb asked. "What are you doing?"

"Coming home from a ride."

Caleb stood there, searching Ephraim's face for a hint of how it'd gone. Ephraim was not forthcoming.

"You took a girl then...?" he finally pressed.

Ephraim began to unhitch the buggy. "Of course."

When Caleb continued standing there, Ephraim stopped what he was doing and faced him. "Why the sudden interest? *Ach,* does this have something to do with the shop? I'm not allowed to go out now? Are you trying to control my entire life?"

Caleb frowned. "I was just asking about your evening."

Ephraim took a step closer and studied Caleb's face. Caleb wanted to snuff out the lantern, but of course, that would be absurd.

"Wait a minute," Ephraim said. "Hold on. You already know who I took riding, and it *bothers* you."

"I-I never said that," Caleb countered, wishing he was upstairs in his room—anywhere but there.

"You *like* her," Ephraim accused with no small amount of glee. "You like Ruth Riehl."

Caleb's nostrils flared, and he couldn't think of one thing to say. His brother was right.

Ephraim put back his head and laughed. Caleb glanced at the house, afraid his father would hear and come out to see what the hilarity was all about.

"Be quiet, would you?" Caleb asked.

"How did you even know I was out with Ruth?" Ephraim's eyes narrowed. "How could you have known?"

"I guessed."

"You *guessed?* Out of all the single girls in Hollybrook, you guessed?"

"Fine. I saw you talking with her."

Ephraim paused. "Oh... You were spying on me."

"I was not."

"But you were," Ephraim said, his words coming fast. "You were out looking for me and you saw me talking with Ruth. A lovely girl, Ruth."

For one mad moment, Caleb wanted to reel back and punch his brother. The urge shocked him so soundly that his mouth dropped open, and he took a quick step backward.

Ephraim was quiet now, but his gaze did not leave his brother's eyes. "So now, I've not only stolen your job, but your girl."

"She's not my girl."

"But you wish she was." Ephraim sighed loudly and went back to unhitching the buggy. "Don't fret, brother. I didn't ask her out again. She's much better suited to you."

Caleb didn't move. "What?"

"You heard me. She's much better suited to you." He sighed again. "She didn't like me much, anyway."

Caleb let out the breath he didn't know he was holding. He hesitated for a moment and then he stepped forward and quietly began helping his brother with the unhitching.

Later, back in his room, Caleb got out his tablet and pencil. He did a bit more figuring on what would be necessary to open his own shop. But now when he thought of it, he saw Ruth involved. He wasn't sure how; he only knew he wanted her to be a part of it. Not only for the business, but for himself. His brother was right.

He liked Ruth Riehl. He liked her a lot.

Chapter Thirteen

Ruth spent the entire morning working on new wind chimes. She only stopped to help customers who came into her shop. Many tarried, watching her work. A few of them asked if she'd give workshops so they could learn to make their own.

"Why, I s'pose I could," she answered the first request.

By the time a third customer asked, her mind was busy working out how she could do it. It would be an additional way to make money, which she liked. Her folks would like that, too, considering she gave most of her profits to them. Not that they needed her profits, especially; it simply was how things worked.

She was surprised when it was lunchtime. She didn't close the shop; she ate her lunch behind the counter between customers. She didn't mind, as she hadn't been in a position to hire someone to help her so she could take a proper lunch break. However, if this class idea took off, she might be able to hire help. She had mixed feelings about it—she'd always done everything herself, and in truth, she liked it all.

But it would be nice not to have to close the shop when she had an errand or two. And maybe, opening classes would enable her to save some money to begin a fund to eventually buy the shop building. *Ach*, but she'd love to stop paying rent.

She was getting out the meatloaf sandwich she'd packed when the bell above the door tinkled. She looked up, surprised to see Caleb standing there. He didn't come further into the store; in truth, he looked surprised to find himself there at all.

"Hello, Caleb," she said, feeling suddenly shy.

"Uh, hello, Ruth."

"Can I ... can I help you?" And then it dawned on her. Maybe he'd come by to cancel their ride that evening—her spirits immediately dropped.

"Umm." He drew in a deep breath.

"You've come to cancel," she said it for him.

He looked stricken. "*Nee*. I haven't. *Ach*, do you want to cancel?"

"I don't want to," she assured him hurriedly. "I thought that's why you came by."

He looked sheepish. "That ain't it." He gave her a helpless smile. "I don't really know why I came by."

They stared at each other, and then they both laughed. Something passed between them, and Ruth felt warm and tingly inside.

"I guess I'll let you get back to your work," he said.

"I was just going to eat."

"You eat while you're working?"

"I do."

He chuckled. "I often do, too. I don't need to, but there's usually something I want to attend to." He sobered. "Maybe I haven't had anything to distract me from my work before."

A silence hung in the air after he spoke, and Ruth cautioned herself not to read too much into his words.

He walked further into the small shop and picked up one of her wind chimes. It was her favorite one—the chimes hung from a carved wooden bird in flight. She hadn't done the carving, but she'd asked the local toymaker in town to make birds for her. He'd made ten for her chimes, and there was only the one left.

"That's my favorite," she murmured.

"I'd like to buy it."

Her brow raised. "You don't have to—"

He smiled. "I want to. It's beautiful. Maybe I'll hang it in my new sto—" He stopped abruptly.

"Your new store? Is that what you were going to say?"

He breathed out in a heavy sigh. "*Jah,* I was. I didn't mean to say it out loud. I've told no one."

"You're opening a new store? A ... buggy store?"

A look of guilt flashed across his face.

"But not here, surely," she continued. "Are you ... are you moving?" She hoped not; oh, how she hoped not.

"I'm thinking to move up north."

"B-but..." she started to protest and then realized she had no reason to protest. How could she say she liked him and wanted him to stay—that maybe they had the possibility of a something together...? So instead, she said, "That's ... interesting."

His gaze was intent on hers. "You ... wouldn't mind if I left?" She blinked rapidly, but before she could answer him, he continued, "*Ach,* forget I said that. Here, ring up my purchase, please. And I'll be on my way."

She rang up the sale on her old-fashioned register and took his money. Something had gone stiff between them, and she wasn't sure how to fix it. But he didn't give her a chance, anyway, for he gave her a quick nod of farewell and headed toward the door.

"I'll ... I'll see you tonight," she called after him.

He nodded again and left the store. She watched the bell tremble above the door and heard its ring fade as he walked out of sight.

Lord, he'd made a mess of that somehow. Caleb looked down at the brown package in his hand. And now he had a new wind chime which he didn't need. But it was pretty; he could give it to his mother for Christmas.

One thing the interlude had made clear: he needed to come clean with his folks. If he was making firm plans to leave Hollybrook, they should know. He cringed at the thought. He didn't really want to deal with his parents in this. But he had fulfilled his obligation to his grandfather. He'd shown Ephraim everything to be shown—and now, it was up to Ephraim. Caleb had no stomach to keep doing everything for his brother. And it hurt to think of leaving Ebersole's Buggies, but it was more distressing to stay.

He was of age to move on—more than of age. It was time he started something of his own.

He worked through the afternoon, keeping his eye on the shop door, hoping Ephraim would show. And he did—at nearly five o'clock.

"I'm here," he announced, walking into the office where Caleb sat.

"I see that." Caleb stood from the desk and moved away from it. "Here. You can have your desk back."

"It's never been my desk, brother," Ephraim said. "No matter how much *Dat* or *Groosdaadi* want it to be."

"You need to know something," Caleb said. "I'm leaving. I'm going north to open my own store. I've narrowed it down to two possible places. I, uh, well, I wanted you to know."

Ephraim sank to the office chair and gaped at him. "What?"

"I've been making plans..."

"I see that. Do ... do our folks know?"

"I'm going to tell them when I get home."

"They're not going to be happy."

He drew in a deep breath. "Probably not."

Ephraim's expression tightened. "So, it's really going to fall to me." He threw out his hand, encompassing the store. "The whole thing."

"That's what *Dat* wants and what *Daadi* wanted. And *Mamm*, too, I s'pose."

"I think I should be the one to leave."

Caleb's jaw clenched. "You can't leave."

"But I can." Ephraim stood. "And I want to. The store is yours. *Dat* can't force it on me, and *Daadi's* gone. I'm sorry I'm to be a huge disappointment to him, but I can't do this. I don't want to do this. And I don't have to."

"But—"

Ephraim shook his head. "Funny how we think we don't have choices, but we do. And I'm choosing."

And with that, he marched out of the office and out of the store. Caleb leaned against the wall. Their father would never accept it. He would never agree to let Ephraim go. It was going to be hard enough for him to leave and go up north—but Ephraim? No. It would never be allowed.

He had the distinct feeling Ephraim was going home right then to announce his decision, and Caleb needed to be there. He hurried out of the office.

"Shannon, take care of things, will you? I don't know if I'll be back today or not. Just close up when it's time."

"Certainly, Caleb. Don't fret. I'll be fine." She gave him a motherly smile, and he wondered fleetingly if she'd heard his conversation with Ephraim.

He strode from the office, went around to hitch the buggy, and hurried for home.

By the time he arrived, Ephraim was already there. Caleb had no idea how, but when he walked into the front room, a confrontation was already underway.

"You won't," Lloyd was saying, his voice already raised a notch.

Caleb saw his mother twisting the edge of her apron, a traumatized look on her face.

"*Dat*, it's useless. Caleb is going to leave, and then what? The store will disappear, that's what. It won't survive Caleb leaving."

Caleb burst into the room, and now Lloyd's and Bernice's eyes were on him.

"What?" Lloyd said. "What's this he's saying?"

"It's true," Caleb said, bracing himself. "I'm planning to move up north and open my own store. It's time. I've shown Ephraim all he needs to know—"

"I'm *not* running the store," Ephraim cried. "I'm sick of telling all of you. Can you not hear me? I don't want the store. I've *never* wanted the store."

"You have to want it," Bernice said, her voice trembling. "What else will you do?"

"I'm going to work with Benjamin at the local café."

"What?" Lloyd cried, his eyes huge. "Waiting tables? They have Susie and Martha for that!"

"I'm going to learn to cook."

"*Cook?*" Lloyd's voice was laced with surprise and anger.

"*Jah.* Cook. I was going to leave, and I still will if I have to. But I want to cook. I've decided."

"You've never shown one inch of interest in cooking," Lloyd cried.

"That's because *Mamm* always chased me out of the kitchen." He looked at Bernice whose mouth had gaped open. "You never let me. You kept forcing me to the shop or out to the fields. But I was always interested. I just never seriously considered it possible before."

"Cook?" Lloyd repeated. "*Nee. Nee.* You'll run the shop."

"Then I'm leaving," Ephraim said. His voice was even, unemotional now. It was as if he'd flipped a switch. He was eerily calm. "I'll go to Linder Creek first and find a job in a restaurant there. If that doesn't work, I'll take to the road again. It shouldn't be that hard to find a place that will take me."

Bernice was sobbing quietly now. Lloyd's eyes remained huge and disbelieving, as if his buggy had just flipped topside.

Ephraim squared his shoulders and headed out of the room, but Bernice jumped to her feet, tears streaming down her cheeks. "*Nee!* You'll go nowhere!" Her voice shook, and she looked as if she could barely get the words out, but her cheeks were flushed and feverish-looking. "You'll work with Benjamin if that's what you want. And Caleb? You'll run my *dat's* shop. It should have been that way from the first. We all knew it. Even *Dat* knew it. And all this—" she threw her arms out, "all this... I won't have my family torn apart. I won't have it!"

She stepped over to where Lloyd was standing, breathing hard. "Lloyd, it's over. *Dat* is gone. Ephraim's been right from the start. It's over. He's not the one for the buggy shop."

Caleb watched his father inhale sharply, and then it was as if someone let out all his air. He sagged and sank to the davenport.

"I'm trying to honor your father," he said, looking up at his wife. "And Ephraim, he needed... He needed..."

"He needs to do what's best for him," Bernie said, her tone resigned. "We were wrong."

Ephraim appeared shock by this turn of events. "All right, *M-mamm*," he said, nearly sputtering. "All right. Okay. Well. Looks like I'll be staying then. *Jah*. I'll stay."

Bernice sat down beside Lloyd and took his hand. Then she cast her eyes upon Caleb.

Caleb felt suddenly weak. He went to a rocker and sat down. "Does this mean... Does this mean Ephraim won't be taking over the buggy shop? Is that truly what you're saying?"

Bernice nodded through her tears. "I won't have my family torn apart."

Lloyd sighed and looked down at his thick, calloused hands. He sighed again and then glanced over at Caleb. "Your *mamm* is right. You'll take over the shop."

Caleb's mind whirled as he tried to discern what he was feeling. Freed? Excited? Stunned? If Ephraim was out of the picture—truly out of the picture, then he would run Ebersole's Buggies. Would he be content with that after spending days planning his own shop?

Wait. His own shop? Wouldn't Ebersole's Buggies become his own shop—at least for all practical purposes?

"So, I would run *Daadi's* shop?" he asked. "As my own?"

Lloyd let out his breath and nodded. "I'm not fighting this anymore. It will be as yours. As it should have been from the start."

"And you're happy with that?"

Lloyd looked at Bernice, and they both looked at him. He could see in the depths of their gazes that they were relieved.

"We're happy with that," his mother said softly. She wiped at her eyes with the corner of her apron.

"All right," he said and stood. He clapped Ephraim on the shoulder, and they stared at each other a long minute.

"Let's go tend the animals," Ephraim suggested, and the two of them turned and walked outside together.

Chapter Fourteen

Caleb hadn't unhitched the buggy. In minutes, he'd be leaving to pick up Ruth. Would she be excited to see him? He hoped so. They'd parted oddly earlier that day, and he supposed that had been his fault. *Ach*, but he'd been a mess lately. But now, he felt so much better. He was even beginning to put together how he could implement some of his ideas for his new shop into Ebersole's Buggies instead.

He was thinking to expand. He could build a small addition that could house all the buggy supplies. He could even add on a shoeing area and hire a man. As it stood now, the only way to get horses shod was to call a traveling farrier, and sometimes Joseph wasn't available for a day or two. Caleb would talk to him—see if there was enough market for two. He certainly didn't want to take Joseph's customers away from him. He figured it'd work, though, because Joseph serviced horses in more than one district, and he didn't live in Hollybrook.

Caleb was aware he was smiling. He hadn't smiled so freely for a long time. *Ach,* but he couldn't wait to tell Ruth everything that had happened. There was another idea percolating in his mind, and he wondered if he should share it with her. He didn't want to seem overbearing, nor did he want to seem presumptuous. But he liked the idea that was forming more and more strongly with each passing minute.

His spirits soaring, he got into the buggy and headed toward the Riehl farm. He was a few minutes early, but he couldn't wait any longer. *Please Gott,* he prayed, *please let Ruth be fond of me. Let her be interested in courtship. Let her want to be with me.*

Funny how quickly a day could change. He would never have guessed earlier he'd be so excited this evening. He would never have guessed things would have taken such a turn and given him such hope.

He was whistling now. When he neared Ruth's place, he slowed the buggy and then pulled to the side of the road. Someone stepped out from the shadows of a young maple tree.

"Ruth," he cried.

Ruth saw him coming from well down the road. He was early. Her breath hitched. Did that mean he was eager to see her? Did that mean he was looking forward to their evening together? Despite their awkwardness earlier, she hoped so. How she hoped so.

After he greeted her, she quickly walked to the buggy and climbed in. There was something different about Caleb that night; it was immediately obvious.

"Something's happened," she said.

He gave her a quizzical look and snapped the reins. "Why do you say that?"

She even heard it in his tone. He was happy. The edge of sadness had fled.

"You're happier. What's happened?"

"You can tell?"

She gave him a light jab in his arm. "Of course, I can. Are you going to tell me?"

"And if I don't?" he teased.

"I'll... I'll..." What would she do? "I'll jump out of this moving buggy, and you'll be sorry."

The silly threat made him laugh. "So, you'll jump right on out. Have a broken leg for Christmas, then?"

She put on her best scowl. "Caleb Ebersole, tell me."

"Maybe I will, or—"

"Fine!" she snapped playfully. "I don't care a fig about what's happened."

But, of course, she did care. It was amazing how much she cared considering they hadn't spent all that much time together. What was it about him that drew her so? What was it about him that made her want to know everything that affected his life?

"I hope you do care," he said, this time more seriously. His tone softened, and she heard the affection in it.

"I do," she said softly. "And it's *gut, ain't so*? Whatever it is that's happened?"

"It's *gut*," he acknowledged. "Ebersole's Buggies... It's mine."

She gaped at him. "Truly? But how?"

"Ephraim wants to be a cook, of all things..." Caleb shrugged. "And *Dat* and *Mamm* agreed. They truly agreed. And so, the buggy shop falls to me."

"Where it should have been all along," she said, her heart soaring at his good news.

His gaze intensified and the buggy slowed. "Thank you for saying that."

"It's true. And how lovely that it happened right at Christmas time."

"Sort of like my Christmas inheritance." He smiled. "I was prepared to move, but now I don't have to."

Her heart opened, and she breathed her silent thanks to God. "*Nee.* Now you don't have to move."

"Are you... Are you ... glad?" She heard the nervousness in his voice.

"I'm glad." Her words came easily, and she meant them with her whole heart.

He sucked in a breath. "*Gut,* because... Well, there's something else."

"Something else *gut?*"

"I hope so."

He seemed so nervous now that she found herself growing nervous, too. What was he going to say? And would she like it?

"Tell me. Hurry up!"

He laughed, and his shoulders visibly relaxed. "*Ach,* Ruth, but I like you."

She gasped lightly as his words filled the buggy. He *liked her.* She pressed her hand to her chest, and her breathing went shallow.

"*Ach,* I didn't mean to say it out like that," he said, but his voice was low and warm and resonant. "But there it is. It's true. I can't stop thinking about you. I'm likely saying way too much, way too soon, but I've done it now. What I want to know is...."

He paused and she held her breath.

"...are you interested in courting?"

She drew in a deep breath, letting his words flow over her and through her. "*Jah*," she said, her eyes burning with happy tears, "*jah*, I am."

He reached over and grabbed her hand, laughing. "Thank you. Thank you."

"No need to thank me," she said, blinking back her tears. "I ... like you, too."

His smile widened even further. "I have some ideas for the shop."

"Tell me."

"I'm thinking to offer farrier services, and there is something else..." He inhaled. "I was thinking about, well, if all goes well between us... I was thinking about expanding the shop to include an area for your wind chimes. Your shop could be connected to the buggy shop."

Her eyes widened. "You mean... If all goes well between us, I wouldn't have to pay rent anymore?"

"That's what I'm thinking."

She laughed. "I like that idea. I like it right fine."

"I'm thirty years old, Ruth."

"I figured you to be around that age…"

"I don't have much interest in drawing a courtship out…" His eyes were bright, compelling.

She smiled. "So… hopefully, that won't be necessary, will it?"

He laughed richly and amusement flickered in his eyes. "*Ach*, Ruth, you are an amazing woman."

Joy bubbled in her heart, and her smile broadened. "And you are an amazing man."

Their gazes locked, and Ruth saw the beginning of a lifetime of love in his eyes. He snapped the reins and the buggy sped up.

"Where shall we go?" he asked.

"I don't care one bit," she answered. "It's enough that we're together."

"*Jah*," he agreed, flashing her a wide, beautiful smile, "it's enough that we're together."

The End

Continue Reading...

Thank you for reading **The Christmas Inheritance. Are you wondering what to read next?** Why not read **The Nanny's Christmas Decision?** Here's a peek for you:

VISIT HERE To Read More!
https://ticahousepublishing.com/amish.html

Thank you for Reading

If you **love Amish Romance**, <u>**Visit Here:**</u>

https://amish.subscribemenow.com/

to find out about all <u>**New Hollybrook Amish Romance Releases! We will let you know as soon as they become available!**</u>

If you enjoyed ***XXXXXX*** would you kindly take a couple minutes to leave a positive review on Amazon? It only takes a moment, and positive reviews truly make a difference. I would be so grateful! Thank you!

Turn the page to discover more Amish Romances just for you!

More Amish Romance for You

We love clean, sweet, rich Amish Romances and have a lovely library of Brenda Maxfield titles just for you! (Remember that ALL of Brenda's Amish titles can be downloaded FREE with Kindle Unlimited!)

If you love bargains, you may want to start right here!

VISIT HERE to discover our complete list of box sets!

https://ticahousepublishing.com/bargains-amish-box-sets.html

VISIT HERE to find Brenda's single titles.

https://ticahousepublishing.com/amish.html

About the Author

I was blessed to live part-time in Indiana, a state I shared with many Amish communities. I now live in Costa Rica. One of my favorite activities is exploring other cultures. My husband, Paul, and I have two grown children and six precious grandchildren. I love to hole up in our mountain cabin and write. You'll also often find me walking the shores by the sea. Happy Reading !

https://ticahousepublishing.com/